Murder, She Floats

(A Damon Lassard Dabbling Detective Mystery)

by

Stephen Kaminski

For information, email **Cozy Cat Press**, cozycatpress@aol.com or visit our website at: www.cozycatpress.com

COZY CAT PRESS

ISBN: 978-1-939816-49-8

Printed in the United States of America

Cover design by Karri Klawiter
http://artbykarri.com/cover-art/e-book-print-cover-art-design/

1 2 3 4 5 6 7 8 9 10

Praise for the Damon Lassard
Dabbling Detective Mysteries

Don't Cry Over Killed Milk

"What a treat! It's fast-paced with likeable characters that work very well together. There's a wonderful blend of mystery and romance. If you are a fan of good old fashioned mysteries that keep you guessing until the last couple of chapters, this is the perfect book for you."

—*Socrates' Cozy Cafe*

"Just when I don't think there could be another unbelievable cozy mystery, I am proven wrong. I had never heard of Amniotic Band Syndrome before I read this book, and I love the fact that this is a mystery with a message. I honestly don't believe I have ever read a mystery that dealt with such serious issues of depression, bullying, and retribution. Again, I was so drawn into this story that I nearly read it all in one sitting. Damon was either diabolically clever, immeasurably stupid, or a splendid combination of the two. I do believe that all loose ends were tied up satisfactorily."

—*My Devotional Thoughts*

"In this the second of author Stephen Kaminski's brilliant series, our amateur sleuth is hard at work on not just one but two mysteries in the charming community of Hollydale. The well-written and complicated twist of events made clear by the end of the book is intriguing, delightful, and down-right entertaining. I also found that the author handles sensitive issues with a deft, yet gentle hand. There is of course the on-going mystery as to whether Damon will choose his best friend Rebecca or that darn weather-girl Bethany! With detective Gerry Sloman and Damon on the case along with all the other people who inhabit their little corner of the world, you are sure to be in for a real treat! Can't wait to read more in this swell series!"

—*Barbara Jean Coast*
Author of the Poppy Cove Mystery series

"Calling all cosy mystery lovers. Damon Lassard is the male equivalent of Jessica Fletcher in Murder, She Wrote. Damon Lassard is a likeable and enthusiastic character. I enjoyed this story; it is a quick, easy, and entertaining read. Even better, it is tightly plotted with a motive which is compelling and has some great original twists. It has been a long time since I have read such an entertaining yet at the same time thoughtful cosy mystery."

—*Cleopatra Loves Books (UK)*

"I thought the book was really good and the characters were likable. The plot was great and well written. He pulled you in right away and kept you interested through the whole story."

—*Shelley's Book Case*

Don't Cry Over Killed Milk by Stephen Kaminski is a fun, well-written, cozy mystery. I really enjoyed Damon Lassard. He was smart and a different type of cozy sleuth than I typically read. I liked having the male perspective. The author kept me guessing with a well-crafted whodunit."

—*Brooke Blogs: Live Laugh, Love, Blog*

It Takes Two to Strangle

"If you enjoy cozy mysteries such as the Hamish MacBeth and Agatha Raisin series by M.C. Beaton and the Coffeehouse series by Cleo Coyle, you'll definitely enjoy your time with *It Takes Two to Strangle*."

—*Dreamworld Book Reviews*

"Using a laid back writing style, with subtle humor, Kaminski engages his reader through carefully delivered dialog, plot preview, revealing nuances, and clues that fortify the storyline. Frequent unexpected plot developments, romantic innuendos, and interaction among the key players engage the reader from the early pages right through to the dramatic finale."

—*Reader Views*

Other Cozy Cat Press Titles by Stephen Kaminski

It Takes Two to Strangle: A Damon Lassard Dabbling Detective Mystery

Winner of the 2012 Reader Views Literary Award— Mid-Atlantic Region

Don't Cry Over Killed Milk: A Damon Lassard Dabbling Detective Mystery

Winner of the 2013 Reader Views Literary Award— Mid-Atlantic Region

Honorable Mention: 2013 Reader Views Literary Award— Mystery/Thriller/Suspense/Horror

2013 Chanticleer Media CLUE Award Finalist

For James and Cheryl

A special thank you to:
Royal Caribbean International®
and
the kind and knowledgeable crew on the
Oasis of the Seas®

Prologue
Tuesday, January 14

Damon Lassard pushed wet thumbs hard into his temples. Confined to a shower stall the size of an upright casket, he allowed steaming water to sear his upper back, and willed his brain to glue a morass of information into a cohesive story. Damon was knee-deep in a "locked boat" mystery.

Similar to the plot of a classic detective novel, a suicide note had been found in the drawer of a locked room. But Damon wasn't visiting a quaint farmhouse in the English countryside. He was on a cruise ship and his dining companion had been spotted floating face-up off the coast of an island in the Bahamas. Damon alone was convinced that there had been unwelcome assistance.

* * *

Sunday, January 12

Two days earlier, on a Sunday afternoon in Miami, Damon boarded the *Vitamin of the Seas* with his mother. Lynne Lassard-Brown was an enthusiastic traveling companion, but was not the person Damon had originally intended as his vacation partner.

In early October, he had started dating Bethany Krims, the beautiful weather girl who lived near him in the Hollydale community of Arlington, Virginia. She had planned to move to Atlanta for a position with a national weather network, but at the last minute, Bethany was informed that the station's talent director had "changed creative direction," and the network rescinded its offer.

Damon had been secretly thrilled. He spent countless hours consoling Bethany, and their friendship blossomed into romance. As a holiday present, Damon booked a mid-January Caribbean cruise. But after the New Year's celebrations died down, so did Bethany's ardor. She broke off their relationship for reasons still unclear to him.

Damon's mother, Lynne, who had overtly been pushing him to take a nonplatonic interest in his best friend, Rebecca, urged him to use the cruise as an opportunity to deepen his relationship with her. But Damon couldn't bring himself to take that step. Instead, he invited his twice-widowed mother to join him on the high seas for seven days of splendor.

Chapter 1
Sunday, January 12

The *Vitamin of the Seas* was a feat of modern engineering; its personnel operations, a logistician's dream. Five thousand passengers boarded the ship, joining two thousand members of the cruise staff. The *Vitamin* stood thirteen decks tall and featured four swimming pools, six theaters, a miniature amusement park, and gardens the size of a public park.

"I've never seen anything like this," Damon said as he hiked up the gangway alongside Lynne.

"I hope there are some good-looking gentlemen on board," Lynne said and poked her son under his ribcage.

Damon swatted at her hand. "Can't you go ten minutes without thinking about men?"

"Why should I?" she teased. "What would make me most happy is for *you* to meet someone on the ship. You're almost thirty-two years old, and you've made it fairly clear that you're not going to make a play for Rebecca anytime soon."

Damon was saved from responding by a professional photographer who stopped them for an obligatory preboarding snapshot. Then they followed a stream of fellow passengers onto the entrance platform of the ship where a tuxedo-clad waiter offered warm greetings and complimentary glasses of champagne.

"You can definitely tell who's been on board one of these ships before," Damon observed as he peered at the sea of passengers around them. "Half of the people are staring in amazement at the chandeliers, and the other half are sprinting inside."

Lynne brought the champagne flute down from her lips. "They're either setting up spa appointments or shore excursions. And I guarantee some are heading straight to the casino—the table games open as soon as we set sail." Lynne had been on a cruise five years earlier with her second husband. She took Damon's elbow. "Let's take a look at our room, and then we can check out the ship."

A glass elevator whisked the pair to the ninth deck. Hundreds of stateroom doors lined either side of a narrow hallway. They dodged porters delivering suitcases on wheeled trolleys, housekeepers steering cleaning carts, and passengers in loud Hawaiian shirts, until they finally reached their stateroom.

"Did I ever tell you about the time I woke up in a hotel room and thought I was covered in blood?" Lynne asked Damon as she opened the door.

"I don't think so," Damon said, looking at his mother curiously. He followed her into the modest-sized room that would serve as their living quarters for the next seven days and scanned its interior. A tiny bathroom and closet flanked the left side of the entryway. The room opened into a wider space with a queen-sized bed, small nightstand, and a blue-fabric sofa lining the left side of the room. Opposite the sofa, a television sat atop a low, curved dresser. A ceiling-to-floor sliding door stood at the end of the room and opened to a small cement balcony.

"It happened twenty years ago, when your father was still alive." Lynne sat down on the sofa and stretched her legs. Despite her fifty-plus years, she often received compliments on her lithe figure. "We left you with your grandparents and went to Chicago for a long weekend. It was the middle of the summer and hot as Hades outside. We spent an exhausting Saturday sightseeing, topped off with an evening musical and a late nightcap. When we returned to our hotel near the Navy Pier, I had to crank up the air conditioning because the room was sweltering."

"No problem with the air in here," Damon said and cracked open the door to the balcony, allowing warm Miami air into the stateroom.

"Thankfully not," Lynne agreed. "Anyway, when I woke up the next morning and went into the bathroom, my face was covered with brown smears. I ran my fingers through my hair and parts of it were stiff." She touched the wispy, low-lighted gray hair that swirled in front of her ears.

"That sounds scary, Mother."

"It was, and I panicked. I remember screaming and running back to the bed. There were stains on my pillow. Your father, who was still half-asleep, started pulling strands of hair away from my scalp, looking for a gash."

Damon raised his eyebrows in anticipation.

Lynne blushed. "He didn't find anything on my head. But he did discover a candy wrapper stuck to the underside of the top sheet. I'd been so worn out the night before that I didn't notice the square of chocolate on my pillow. The room's heat softened it before I turned on the air conditioning. Your father and I sure had a good laugh."

* * *

Damon and Lynne admired the view from their stateroom balcony as the *Vitamin* set sail, then spent the next three hours exploring the ship. Towering rock-climbing walls and a zip line offered thrills for adventure-seekers. Wine bars, art galleries, and a library nestled alongside the park provided cozy spots of respite. An enormous Fun-Zone was equipped with an arcade, science lab, and two-dozen staffers to babysit toddlers and coordinate activities for children and teens. And a five-hundred-foot-long promenade boasted a glut of lounges, live musicians, and high-end retail shops.

When booking the cruise, Damon had selected a traditional dining experience. During breakfast and lunch, he and Lynne would fight the masses at enormous buffets. In the evenings, however, they had "first seating" reservations in the Pelican Room, one of three large but upscale dining rooms aboard the ship.

Dressed in smart, casual clothing, Damon and Lynne entered the Pelican Room at six thirty. A small line had formed at the entry for mandatory hand sanitizing. A crew member jockeying a Purell dispenser explained that the ship had had an outbreak of norovirus the previous week. In response, this week's passengers were required to disinfect before entering any of the dining areas. And the breakfast and lunch buffets wouldn't be self-service—instead, crew members working overtime would dish out portions of nourishment.

Once past the sanitizing station, a formally dressed headwaiter introduced himself to Damon and Lynne as Charles. He stood about two inches taller than Damon's lanky six-foot-one inch frame and bore a black horseshoe moustache.

During the booking process, Damon had been informed that a majority of the dining room tables were set for twelve. He and his mother would have a group of companions for the week and the same waiters each night.

Charles led Damon and Lynne to a table near the rear of the Pelican Room. Velvet drapes, oak wainscoting, and dim lighting gave the room a somber appearance. When they reached the table, three men rose from their seats. Five ladies remained sitting.

Charles said with a flourish, "Ms. Lynne Lassard-Brown and her son, Mr. Damon Lassard." The thick-jowled headwaiter turned and hurried off to greet new arrivals at the front of the dining room.

A bearded gentleman who appeared to be in his seventies strode around the table and shook Damon's hand firmly. He kissed Lynne on the cheek and introduced himself as Houston Drummiller. A well-tailored suit couldn't disguise his corpulence.

"Welcome to our table," Houston said with vigor. "My family has been taking these cruises for years, and we always enjoy meeting new people. Let me introduce everyone."

He first presented his wife, Kitty, who looked to be in her early seventies. Her heavily plucked eyebrows accentuated a high forehead. A tree-trunk waistline belied her name. She proffered a flaccid hand to Damon but didn't rise.

Next to Kitty stood Miles Drummiller, Houston and Kitty's son. "It's a pleasure to meet you both," he said. Miles had a ruddy complexion and broad shoulders, but his muscular build was making a natural progression to fat.

The table was circular and its chairs were arranged like a clock, with Houston at the twelve o'clock-position. Silverware gleamed against burgundy napkins and a crisp white tablecloth. At the three o'clock position sat Philippa Drummiller, Miles's wife. She nodded curtly in turn to Lynne and Damon. Philippa reminded Damon of a prom queen who hadn't aged well. Her mouth was fixed in a dour expression that suggested she didn't relish the thought of spending the next seven nights with people of Damon's caste. *Her necklace probably cost more than my car,* Damon thought.

Before Damon and Lynne could meet the remaining four diners, a booming, "Howdy folks," rang out from behind them. The attention of every person at the table turned to a craggy-faced man standing arm in arm with a devastatingly beautiful young woman. She had blue eyes so clear Damon could see through them. Her dark-brown hair was pulled back into a tony loose ponytail that cascaded around her left shoulder, the tendrils grazing the swell of her breasts. Damon's breath caught.

"Looks like we'll be joining y'all for dinner this week," the man said. "I'm Jack Jackman from Dallas, and this here is my best girl, Fava."

Damon's brain raced. Was Fava the man's daughter or a trophy girlfriend? She looked about thirty.

As the couple walked around the table, shaking hands, Lynne winked at Damon. He knew she could read his mind.

Damon introduced himself to Jack and Fava. His eyes lingered on Fava's for a second longer than social graces permitted, but Jack didn't appear to notice. He seemed too busy appraising Lynne's finer attributes.

"Do you live in Dallas as well?" Damon asked Fava. If the answer was "no," there was a chance she was Jack's daughter.

"Of course, silly," she replied playfully and touched Damon's wrist. "That's where Jack and I met."

Damon's spirits sank.

Lynne overheard and steered Damon to the remainder of their new tablemates. They met Raymond and Vicky Carmichael. Raymond, who had thin lips and a gap between his top front teeth, was Houston Drummiller's godson. His wife, Vicky, stood as Damon approached, showing off a kitschy, ruffled dress covered in wallpaper flowers and shoes too sensible for the occasion. When Damon reached for her hand, he expected a vapid shake but instead received an overt two-handed caress. Damon wrenched back his hand.

Vicky and Raymond had seats in the four and five o'clock positions around the table. At six and seven, two younger women sat. The older of the pair, who was smartly dressed, introduced herself as Amanda Drummiller-Sweet, Houston and Kitty's daughter. The younger was Miles and Philippa's daughter, Candice. Both wore diamond-studded watches and heavy gold bracelets.

Two more Drummillers, Damon thought. That made six at the table for twelve. Eight, if you counted Raymond and Vicky. Damon considered Amanda and her niece, Candice. In her midthirties, Amanda had a mischievous playfulness behind her eyes. Full lips and high cheekbones gave her an alluring quality despite an obvious resemblance to Houston. Candice looked like an expensively clad, gothic version her mother. She didn't share Philippa's sour-grapes countenance, but appeared bored by her company.

A pair of waiters wearing matching black-and-white garb approached, and the assemblage of diners took their places at the table. Damon sat in the eight o'clock position between Amanda and his mother. Jack took the seat to Lynne's left. Fava sat between him and Houston. Damon pictured Jack clutching one of Fava's perfectly shaped knees under the table.

"Welcome to the *Vitamin of the Seas*," one of the waiters said. His back was ramrod straight and his scalp, freshly waxed. "My name is Niels. I'll be your primary waiter this week."

"Where are you from, Niels?" Kitty asked.

"I'm originally from Rotterdam in the Netherlands," he replied. Niels nodded at his companion. "This is Kristjan from Estonia. He'll be your assistant waiter."

The young Baltic man bowed his head silently and stepped a pace behind the senior waiter.

"Estonia, huh?" Jack said. "I used to do business with a company over there. In Tallinn. I imported electronics equipment from them. Good people, the Estonians."

Kristjan smiled and blushed.

Fava poked Jack in the chest with a french-tipped fingernail. "Stop it," she said. "You're embarrassing him."

"Just being friendly, darling." He kissed her cheek. Damon noticed Fava flinch as his cracked lips brushed her smooth skin.

After Niels and Kristjan filled water glasses, Houston ordered two bottles of wine for the table.

"Looks like you have quite a crew here, Houston," Jack said. "Is there a special occasion?"

Houston puffed out his cheeks. "We take these little trips quite often, but tomorrow does happen to be my granddaughter's twenty-first birthday."

Candice rolled her eyes. "It's not as if I did anything special."

"Come now, Candice," Philippa said coolly. "You're doing so well at school, and you've grown past your—"

Candice stared daggers at her mother.

"Get off her case, Philippa," Amanda snapped.

Lynne flashed a large smile at Candice. "We'll have to make sure your dessert has candles in it tomorrow night," she said, obviously recognizing the makings of a familial spat and trying to cut it short. "What are you studying?"

Candice managed a weak smile. "Botany."

"But we all hope she'll join the family business when she graduates," Houston said and gave his son, Miles, a nod.

"She'll have to—a person can't make any money as a gardener or farmer or whatever one does with a botany degree," Philippa said.

Candice clenched her teeth.

Amanda opened her mouth, but Lynne stepped back in. "Anyone can have a fulfilling life if they enjoy what they do. One of the happiest men I know is a parsley famer who couldn't make ends meet." She paused and smiled puckishly. "He never stopped whistling, even after they garnished his wages."

Houston looked at Lynne for a moment, then erupted with laughter. The other men at the table joined him. Vicky Carmichael's face held a puzzled look, clearly not recognizing the play on words.

"So what's the family business?" Damon asked Miles. The tense moment had passed.

"Cardboard," Miles said with pride. "Dad started forty years ago in Rocky Mount, North Carolina, and it's grown ever since. Our factories produce more boxes than anyone else on the East Coast."

"Seems like you've done pretty well for your family," Jack piped in, his eyes set on the Drummiller women's jewelry.

"Years of hard work and dedication have paid off," Houston said. Kitty placed her hand over her husband's.

"And we're still expanding," Miles added. He tried to imitate his father's confident tone, but the words came out with the bluster of a blowhard. Raymond Carmichael's thin lips pursed as he stared at Miles.

"So how do you make cardboard?" Damon asked.

Miles spent the next twenty minutes detailing the manufacturing process and the differences between corrugated cardboard and paperboard. During the exposition, Niels and Kristjan brought appetizers, then main courses, to the table.

Halfway through their entrées, Jack Jackman spat up blood.

Chapter 2

Jack launched a half-inch sliver of glass from his mouth. The bloodied shard landed in a ceramic gravy boat.

"Oh my gosh," Fava shouted. "Jack, are you all right?"

Jack coughed, and blood spilled from his mouth onto his plate. It slithered among the beef Wellington, mashed potatoes, and asparagus like lava finding recesses in rocky terrain. Jack swept a cloth napkin from his lap and crammed it into his mouth.

Houston rose to his feet and yelled for help. Niels sprinted across the dining room, followed by Kristjan and the mustachioed headwaiter, Charles.

Jack gathered a small clump of unswallowed food from his mouth into his napkin, wadded it up, and set it on the table. He snatched Fava's napkin from her outstretched hand and pressed it firmly against the inside of his right cheek.

"That little spear was smack in the middle of my mashed potatoes," Jack said through a mouthful of napkin. He pointed at the glistening spike floating in rich, brown gravy.

Charles and the waiters rushed to a stop beside Jack. Their eyes followed his finger and focused on the shard of glass in the gravy boat.

"My most sincere apologies, sir," Charles gushed. "Let me clean this up and get you a fresh entrée." He reached for Jack's plate.

Jack caught Charles's arm in midair. "Not so fast."

The headwaiter's face registered shock. "You'd prefer me to leave the plate, sir?" he asked. "I assure you it's no trouble at all. Besides, there's blood all over your food."

Jack's wrinkled eyes narrowed. He removed the red-splotched napkin from his mouth and tossed it on the table. Without removing his grip from Charles's arm, he turned to Fava. "Do you have your camera in your purse, dear?"

Fava looked just as confused as Charles. But she answered, "Of course. You know I carry it everywhere."

Jack smiled. "Be a good girl and take photographs of everything here. That shard of glass in the gravy boat, my plate, both of our napkins, and the inside of my mouth." He looked at Kristjan. "Go find one of the ship's doctors. I need him to document the lacerations inside my cheek." Jack focused on his tablemates. "If you all don't mind, could I trouble each of you for a written statement, detailing exactly what you witnessed here?" He picked up his fork and delicately pushed around the bloodied food on his plate. The sight was repulsive, and Kitty turned away. But every other set of eyes around the table watched in horrified amazement as Jack pulled a second fragment of glass from the depths of his whipped potatoes.

Jack turned his head toward Niels and Charles. To Niels, he said, "I suggest you collect the other waiters and remove the plates from anyone else who ordered potatoes." Then he directed his attention to Charles, finally releasing the man's arm. "And *you* tell the captain to put in a call to corporate headquarters. They'll want to get their lawyers up to speed. Had I swallowed that sliver of glass, it would have torn up my insides. I could have internally bled to death."

* * *

"What are everyone's evening plans?" Kitty asked politely as her fellow diners finished eating as rapidly as possible within the bounds of etiquette. Every person at the table, other than Jack and Fava, miraculously had somewhere to be that took precedence over dessert. Damon and Lynne used the excuse that there was a musical they were longing to see.

The ship's theater company was, in fact, performing *Evita*. Damon and Lynne found a pair of seats near the back of the twelve-hundred-seat auditorium's upper deck.

"I feel bad for Jack," Lynne whispered as the production started.

"It didn't seem like he was hurt too badly," Damon responded quietly. "The rest of dinner sure was awkward. Everyone in the dining room was staring at us."

"That was Houston's fault more than anyone's. He's the one who shouted. Jack never raised his voice." Damon thought he saw a twinkle in his mother's eye.

"Jack was downright rude to the staff," Damon said. "You don't think grabbing the headwaiter's arm contributed to the stir?"

Lynne looked down at her feet.

"Mother, if I didn't know better, I'd say you were taken by Jack Jackman." Damon frowned. "He's in his sixties and has a trophy girlfriend. Why would you want to get involved with him?"

A woman sitting directly in front of Damon whipped her head around and shushed him. Her chartreuse hat fell forward.

Damon caught it and, handing it back, mouthed an apology. He and Lynne turned their attention to the performance. The acting and singing were tremendous.

During intermission, Damon leaned in close to Lynne. "I've been thinking. Jack sure knew how to handle that situation."

"So?" Lynne asked defensively.

"You *are* smitten with him," Damon said with a smile.

"He has a certain charm. I suppose it's his confidence. And don't think I didn't notice you sizing up Fava. Maybe together we can split the two of them up and keep the parts for ourselves!" Lynne laughed. "As if I could rival that beauty."

"Mother, you draw in men wherever you go. It wouldn't surprise me if you could best a woman half your age."

Lynne pinched his shoulder.

"Okay, a little more than half," Damon said. "But seriously, didn't it seem like Jack knew exactly what to do a bit too well? Photos, witness statements, the whole nine yards."

"I think you've become too involved in mysteries. You're trying to craft something to detect that simply isn't there. We all saw Jack cut himself. He spat a bloody shard of glass out of his mouth for goodness' sake."

In the past year, Damon had helped his friend Detective Gerry Sloman of the Arlington County police force solve two murders. Damon's instincts were so keen that months earlier, Gerry had suggested he go through the local police academy and join the force. Damon had ultimately decided it would be a good idea, despite being asked by the CEO of a commercial real estate company—at almost the exact same time—to join his team.

A few years back, Damon had made a sizable amount of money as a spokesperson for a Japanese chewing-gum company after a mediocre stint with a professional baseball league in Sapporo. Since returning to the States and moving to Hollydale three years ago, he'd slipped into a comfortable but lackluster lifestyle. Living frugally off of interest from his savings, Damon volunteered at the Hollydale library three days a week, served as the local citizens association president, and joined a county crime-solvers group, which passed anonymous tips along to the police. But his days had grown tedious, and Damon longed for regular excitement. So he was looking forward to basic training, which would begin in four weeks.

Damon shifted in his theater seat and looked at his mother, who was picking her cuticles. "I suppose one of the kitchen crew will find a broken glass in the trash next to the line cook who was mashing potatoes. The poor guy will probably get fired."

"That would be unfortunate," Lynne said. "But it's hard to condone negligence."

* * *

After the musical ended, Damon and Lynne stopped by the Crooner—one of thirty-plus drinking establishments on board. The nightspot rested on the sixth deck overlooking the promenade. It was filled with a middle-aged crowd. Couples and foursomes flocked to low, brass-colored tables surrounded by comfortable chairs. A small gathering of singles crowded in front of a U-shaped bar being tended by a pair of men wearing satin-banded fedoras. A band of revelers near a grand piano was collectively belting out "Sweet Caroline" in time to the music. Interior glass portholes with ship etchings, dark wood walls, and thick-matted, blue carpet completed the decor.

Damon ordered drinks at the bar and brought them to Lynne, who had secured a table near a relatively quiet rear corner. Before Damon could say a word, Lynne started to wave. Damon turned to see Miles and Philippa Drummiller.

Miles returned Lynne's wave and pulled his wife toward them. Philippa feigned a smile as they approached. "Nice to see you," she said with spurious sincerity.

"Won't you join us?" Lynne replied sweetly.

"It would be our pleasure," Miles said. He clanked a pair of martini glasses down onto the table. Looking at Damon, he asked, "Can you believe old Jackman nearly impaled his esophagus?"

Philippa gave Miles a stern look. "That was disgusting, and this cruise ship should be ashamed of itself. It's certainly not the type of subject I want to discuss over an evening cocktail." As she sat, Philippa pulled a pashmina shawl from her shoulders and draped it over her knees. Massive teardrop-shaped diamond earrings hung from each side of her oblong face like balances on the scales of justice.

"All right then," Miles allowed, "Damon, tell us about yourself." He shoved two fingers into his drink and plucked out an olive.

Damon provided the curious pair an abbreviated version of his life story.

"So you're basically a layabout," Philippa stated matter-of-factly when he finished.

Damon opened his mouth to retort but gritted his teeth instead.

"I'd say Damon's a man who's been quite successful and is enjoying the fruits of his labor," Miles said. *He didn't sound convinced of his words; perhaps,* Damon thought, *Miles took pleasure in challenging his wife's insults.*

"Damon is signed up to join the police force after the cruise," Lynne chirped.

"The police academy," Damon corrected.

"That sounds positively barbaric to me," Philippa said and curled her lips tightly.

"Well, I think it's admirable, Damon," Miles said. He leaned across the table, and his neck fat lurched like a turkey scrambling away from buckshot. "We need people who work for the social good. I'd do it myself, but I'm too busy growing an empire. I have to keep Philippa here in the Tiffany's-of-the-month club."

The foursome finished their drinks over small talk. Seven hours later, Philippa Drummiller's dead body was found floating upright off the coast of Nassau.

Chapter 3
Monday, January 13

Damon woke at seven fifteen in the morning. The *Vitamin* had docked overnight in Nassau, the capital of the Bahamas, but passengers wouldn't be allowed to deboard for another two hours. Damon quietly slipped on running gear and snuck out of the cabin without waking his mother.

Mild morning air filled Damon's lungs as he began a warm-up jog on the empty track circling the perimeter of the fifth deck. Dawn was a quiet time on board—most passengers slept in after spending a late night in the ship's bars and clubs. But rounding the track near the ship's rear on the starboard side, Damon saw a cluster of people at the top of an open-air staircase that climbed to the sixth deck.

Curious, Damon scrambled up the steps, which ended on the backside of an outdoor aquatics theater. He emerged in a tight space filled with people behind one of a pair of enormous projection screens that straddled the theater's stage. The span between the back of the screen where Damon stood and the ship's rear railing was less than ten feet wide, a shuffleboard court painted on its wooden floorboards. Damon took in the composition of the congregation—security guards, white-coated medical staff, early-rising passengers holding disposable coffee cups, several other joggers, and a pair of men dressed in wetsuits and goggles.

Damon approached the joggers. As he opened his mouth to speak, a loud voice barked, "Who's in charge here?"

Damon turned his head, but his view was completely obscured by a projection screen—it stood over fifteen feet high and twenty-five feet across. He moved with the rest of the crowd toward the stage between the two screens and saw four men marching through the theater's center aisle. Their ornately emblazoned, rust-colored police uniforms clashed with rows of teal seating. The leader of the pack reached the group standing on the stage and shouted, "I am Ibrahim Albury, inspector with the Royal Bahamas Police Force. Is the captain here?"

A ginger-haired man in his sixties who'd been standing at the ship's rail took a step toward the inspector. Worry lines creased his brow. "I'm the captain." He frowned and looked back over the side, toward the ocean.

Damon stepped past the joggers to the waist-high rail. Bobbing in the water, ten feet from the ship's stern, was Philippa Drummiller's lifeless body. Her eyes stared up at him, open and glassy.

"That's Philippa!" Damon exclaimed.

The captain jerked his head in Damon's direction. "You know this woman?" He had a Scandinavian accent.

"Y-Yes," Damon stammered. "I met her yesterday. She's at my dinner table, and she and her husband had a drink with me last night."

"What's her name?" the captain asked.

"Philippa Drummiller."

"All right." Inspector Albury pointed at his deputies. "Get all of the passengers and crew out of here and cordon off this part of the deck. Leave the captain, the medics, the two divers, and that jogger who identified the body." He nodded toward Damon.

The Bahamian police corralled the onlookers and shuttled them away. Damon stayed put. He watched the divers fasten a pulley system to the side of the ship and attach a stretcher to it. Then they walked briskly away from the rear of the deck, presumably to an elevator so they could enter the water at a spot closer to sea level.

Damon considered his location. Rock-climbing walls rose three stories high on both sides of the massive aquatics theater. Several levels of stateroom suites had interior window views of the theater, but the shades were drawn on most. *It probably didn't matter,* Damon thought. Assuming Philippa hadn't floated too far in one direction or the other, if she'd fallen overboard behind one of the projection screens, no one would have seen her. *But had Philippa fallen?* She wasn't drunk when he and Lynne left her and Miles at the Crooner. The couples parted just before midnight. Damon knew the ship had been scheduled to pull into port at one o'clock in the morning. So between one and whatever time her body was first spotted, Philippa had died.

Damon anticipated seeing the body with a morbid eagerness. He couldn't see any blood from six decks up, but if she had been bludgeoned on the back of the head before being tossed overboard, he'd know her demise was no accident. Damon wouldn't be surprised if Philippa had been murdered. She didn't appear to get along with her own daughter. And if Philippa's rudeness to him was indicative of her personality, Damon imagined any of her family members might have had reason to snuff out her last breath.

"Penny for your thoughts, son?" the captain asked Damon. A brass pin on his jacket said "Harris."

"To be honest, sir, I was wondering if she fell by accident or if someone threw an already-dead body overboard." Damon spotted the two divers swimming toward Philippa's body from the side of the ship. A medic started to lower the stretcher.

"People have fallen off of cruise ships before. Usually when they're intoxicated. Though it's never happened on one of mine. From what I hear, there are usually so many people around that the emergency team can jump into rescue mode almost immediately." Captain Harris scratched his chin. "But way back here behind the screen? The theater area is deserted overnight—no one would have heard her scream for help. And if she hit her head on the side of the ship as she fell, she could have been knocked unconscious."

"So even if she has a gash on her head, we wouldn't know if someone hit her because it could have come from the side of the ship," Damon said, then asked, "Would her body float if she drowned?"

Inspector Albury stepped closer to the pair. "Yes, she would float," he said. "We're in salt water, and she doesn't look too muscular from up here." A neatly groomed mustache and beard circled his blanched lips.

As two medics hoisted the stretcher, Albury took down Damon's information and the names of Philippa's family members. Damon included Houston's godson, Raymond Carmichael, and his wife, Vicky, for good measure.

"After I inspect the body, I'll need to speak with the woman's husband, this Miles Drummiller," Albury said looking down at his notes. "And search her quarters." He directed his attention to Captain Harris. "Please find me their stateroom number."

Harris pulled a walkie-talkie from his pants pocket and spoke into it quickly while the medical team deftly lifted the stretcher with Philippa's lifeless body over the railing and onto the deck's floor.

Inspector Albury pushed the medics aside and stood over the body. "Don't try to revive her. The woman's clearly dead." Albury squatted in front of Philippa's face. After a long and silent moment, he tipped her head to one side and then the other. "No sign of blunt force," he said to one of his deputies who had returned from cordoning off the area. "Based on the condition of her face, it looks like she ingested a mass quantity of water and drowned. I suspect this woman didn't know how to tread water."

Albury pointed at Captain Harris. "Let's go find the husband." He nodded at Damon. "You can verify that we have the correct person."

Damon and the captain followed Inspector Albury as he strode out of the aquatics theater, through an outdoor boardwalk-type area complete with a large carousel, and toward a pair of elevator banks, each with six elevators, serving the aft end of the ship.

"Will we be able to finish the cruise?" Damon asked Captain Harris as they walked.

"Most likely," he said. "I'll send news of Mrs. Drummiller's passing to headquarters, of course. But as long as the inspector deems her death to be an accident, we'll continue on. Every now and again, a person dies of natural causes on a cruise ship. It stands to reason—many of our passengers are retirees. Usually, the deceased's family members leave the ship and arrange for the body to be flown home. But occasionally, they ask if we can accommodate transport. We can—every ship in our fleet has a cold storage locker built just for that purpose, and we require the ship's doctors to have training in embalming. The body just goes along for the journey from port to port until we hit our arrival point." He paused, then added quietly to Damon, "If, on the other hand, the inspector suspects foul play, the ship and any suspects will be grounded in the Bahamas for a while. The rest of the passengers will have to find flights home from Nassau."

As Inspector Albury, Captain Harris, and Damon approached an open elevator door, the captain's walkie-talkie squawked. Damon held the door while Harris had a quick conversation. The captain finished and shoved the handheld device into his pocket, stepped inside the elevator, and punched the button for the eleventh deck.

"I have the stateroom number," Harris said. "Actually, numbers—the deceased woman and her husband were staying in separate rooms, albeit side by side with one another."

Clearly Miles and Philippa were not on the best terms, Damon thought to himself.

* * *

Inspector Albury rapped sharply on the door of stateroom 11212. Fifteen seconds later, a yawning Miles Drummiller cracked open the door. He wore loose-fitting boxer shorts under an open bathrobe. Miles rubbed sleep from his eyes. "Can I help you?"

"Are you Mr. Miles Drummiller, husband of Philippa Drummiller?" Albury asked.

"Yes." Miles widened the scope of his gaze, taking in Captain Harris and Damon.

"Your wife, sir, is deceased. She was spotted just before seven a.m., floating alongside the ship."

"What?" Miles blurted.

"She's dead," Albury repeated flatly.

"Did you call the Coast Guard?" Miles shouted. "Surely the paramedics can revive her."

"This is not the United States, sir. And there is no need for the Bahamian equivalent of the Coast Guard. Or medical attention for that matter. Your wife drowned. May I come inside and ask you a few questions?"

Miles looked quickly over his shoulder. "No," he said, clearly flustered. "Where's her body? How do you know it's her?" He pulled the door open another inch.

Captain Harris stepped forward. "Mr. Drummiller, I'm the captain of this ship." He nodded at Damon. "Mr. Lassard here was out jogging this morning while we were preparing to retrieve your wife's, eh, body. He identified Philippa."

Miles gaped at Damon.

"Her body is being held in a secure location," Harris continued. "Once the police are through, we can release her to you in Nassau or we can carry her with us until we finish the week in Miami."

Miles's face whitened. "Let me speak with the rest of my family. They've all been looking forward to this vacation, and today is my daughter's twenty-first birthday." His hand shot to his mouth. "How am I going to tell Candice?" He glanced back into the room. "Give me a minute," Miles said and shut the door. Damon sensed that another person was in the room.

While they waited, Inspector Albury drew a pad of paper from his pocket and began taking notes.

Miles appeared three minutes later wearing plaid shorts and a foam-green, Brooks Brothers polo shirt. He stomped past the three men, closing the stateroom door firmly behind him. Two doors down, he knocked loudly. "Candice?" he shouted, "It's your father. I need to speak with you. Right now!"

Amanda opened the door. Unkempt hair and the absence of makeup softened her natural features. "Miles, it's a bit early. Candice is still asleep."

Miles shoved his way past his sister and shut the door, pushing her into the hall.

Amanda's face registered shock at the abrupt dismissal. "This is my room, too," she yelled to the closed door. Amanda was wearing a bronze-colored tank top and tiny cotton shorts. Damon stepped toward her.

"Damon?" Amanda wrinkled her brow. "What are you doing here?" She looked at the inspector and captain. "What the hell is going on?" she asked, wrapping her arms in front of her bare navel.

Damon looked up and down the hallway. It was empty. "Your sister-in-law, Philippa, died," he said quietly.

Amanda stared at him, wide-eyed.

"Her body was found this morning floating next to the ship," Damon continued.

Amanda exhaled loudly and swiped a strand of chocolate-colored hair from her eyes. "Did she fall overboard?"

Before Damon could answer, Inspector Albury said, "I need to inspect Philippa Drummiller's stateroom."

Damon turned as Harris removed a key card from his wallet. "It's a master," the captain explained and moved to the door directly between Miles's room and the one in which Amanda and Candice were staying.

Albury held up a hand and tried Philippa's door handle. It was locked.

"How many key cards will open this door?" Albury asked Harris.

"Let's see," Harris said and ran a hand through his wavy hair. "Myself and the first officer have master keys that open the doors to all of the rooms. The stateroom attendant—that's the housekeeper—for this stretch of hallway would have a working key card, as would her supervisor. And typically we give two cards to each passenger."

"Who is the first officer?" Albury demanded.

"His name's Eric Fraser."

"And the housekeepers?"

Harris pulled out his walkie-talkie and spoke into it. They waited in silence for a response. Damon could hear sounds of muffled crying coming from inside Candice and Amanda's room. Damon eyed Amanda. She was still covering her midriff, though Damon suspected she had bikinis in her cabin that covered less surface area than her tank top and shorts.

A voice came through Harris's walkie-talkie. Seconds later, the captain said, "The stateroom attendant is Eva Ricaurte and her supervisor is Daniela Montalvo," He spelled their names for Albury. "They are very nice women. From Ecuador."

"Both of them?" Damon asked.

"Yes. We encourage crew from the same country to work together," Harris explained. "We've found that it promotes solid working relationships."

"Okay, six keys," Albury said. He unlatched his own walkie-talkie from a belt loop and radioed to one of his officers. "See if the deceased woman has any key cards in her pockets." Damon recalled that Philippa had been wearing high-end jeans and a cardigan when she was lifted out of the water—a different ensemble than she'd been wearing at the Crooner the night before.

Albury shifted his attention back to the group in the hallway and motioned for the captain to insert his master key into Philippa's door. Other than the color, Harris's key card looked identical to the SeaPass cards passengers used to open their staterooms and to buy drinks on board. "Stay here," the inspector said to Captain Harris and Amanda. Albury pointed to Damon. "I need a neutral witness. That means no one from the ship's staff or family of the deceased. Step inside the room with me but no touching. What's your name again?"

"Damon Lassard, sir."

"If I'm going to be left in the hall, can I at least have something of Philippa's to cover myself with?" Amanda asked. Damon, who had stepped into the room with Albury, pointed to a robe hanging on a hook inside the bathroom's open door.

"No. I said don't touch anything," Albury commanded and slammed the stateroom door shut. The inspector and Damon were alone inside the dead woman's cabin.

* * *

Albury stretched latex gloves over his meaty hands and handed a pair to Damon. "Put these on, but just watch me."

The Bahamian crossed the room to an interior door that connected to Amanda and Candice's cabin. There was no such door linking Philippa's room to Miles's on the opposite side. Albury grasped the handle, but the door was locked. The inspector jotted a note on his pad then walked slowly around the small room. It mirrored Damon's own cabin except there was no balcony—surprising given the family's wealth. Instead, a large modern porthole looked out to sea. "Does that window open?" Damon asked.

Inspector Albury turned and glared at Damon. Apparently, he wasn't allowed to speak either. But the inspector made good on his title and inspected the window. "It would take a sledgehammer to open this window," he stated.

Albury surveyed the top of the dresser and picked up a key card. He delicately placed it into a clear bag he removed from a pocket. "You will note as a witness that I collected one key card," the inspector said to Damon.

A voice crackled through Albury's walkie-talkie. "We found a key card in … dead woman's … pants pocket."

"Put it in an evidence bag," Albury said to the officer on the other end of the transmission. "Was there anything else on her person?"

"A paper note … water-logged … ink ran everywhere … can't make out … words."

"Cursed static," Albury said to himself, then spoke into the walkie-talkie. "Thank you. Keep her things together." He clicked off the communications device.

The inspector spent the next fifteen minutes examining each of the dresser drawers, the sleeper sofa, the closet, and the bathroom. He didn't appear to find anything of significance.

A loud knock interrupted the silence in the room.

"What's going on in there?" Houston Drummiller bellowed from the hallway. Inspector Albury opened the door to the hall. Damon could see the Drummiller family hovering in a pack—Houston, Kitty, Miles, Amanda, Candice, and Raymond. Vicky was noticeably absent. To one side, Captain Harris stood with two women in housekeeping attire and a man in dress uniform whom Damon assumed was the first officer, Eric Fraser.

"Captain," Albury said, ignoring Houston. "I expect to be finished in the next ten minutes. Would you kindly take the family and the ship's crew who have key cards that unlock this room to a secluded area? I'd like to speak with them all after I finish in here."

"Yes, sir," Harris said. "I have a conference room we can use. It's adjacent to the ship's bridge." He gave Albury directions.

"What's *he* doing in there?" Raymond asked, pointing at Damon.

"Acting as an independent witness," Albury replied stiffly. "It is proper protocol to ensure that an inspection can never be second-guessed." He shut the door to the hall and resumed his examination of Philippa's cabin.

After searching the bed, the final item Inspector Albury considered was Philippa's nightstand. It had a single drawer above a small cabinet. A telephone and stationary pad rested on top. Albury opened the drawer and poked his gloved fingers inside, appearing to push something to the side. He stared downward for a solid ten seconds.

"Please come here," he said to Damon.

Damon stepped to Albury's side and peered into the drawer. The inspector carefully picked up a Bible and set it on top of the nightstand. Underneath was a small square of paper with a computer-printed message:

"The world has not been kind to me. I have a cheating husband, wicked daughter, and Houston Drummiller can rot in hell. I leave this life with a clear conscience."

The statement was followed by Philippa's name in type.

The inspector picked up the note and placed it into an empty evidence bag. He quickly scanned the innocuous contents in the nightstand's cabinet, then said, "Well, that's that."

"What do you mean?" Damon asked.

Albury looked Damon in the eye. "What I mean is that this woman clearly took her own life. Mrs. Philippa Drummiller wrote a suicide note and threw herself overboard after the ship docked in port last night."

"How can you be sure?" Damon asked, figuratively donning his amateur detective hat. "The note was typed. Anyone could have done that."

"Because there are only six key cards to this room. One I found on the dresser. One my deputy found in the deceased woman's clothing. The other four are with the ship's crew. I will verify for good measure that none of those cards was stolen. I can't imagine any have been—there are thousands of dollars' worth of jewelry in the dresser. Once verified, I will rule Mrs. Drummiller's death a suicide. The murder rate in the Bahamas is on its way down, thanks to me. I have no intention of adding to the country's homicide numbers when there's no evidence of foul play and I found a suicide note in a deceased woman's locked room."

"But if she invited someone into her room yesterday, that person could have slipped the note in her drawer," Damon protested.

"You've read too many detective stories, Mr. Lassard," Albury said. "That is not the way real crime happens. Murderers either shoot their victims or stab them. And Mrs. Drummiller had no signs of injury."

Chapter 4

Damon and Albury ascended a staircase near the front of the ship to the twelfth deck. Following the directions the captain had provided, they snaked through a warren of narrow hallways that—based on the silver-colored plates mounted on the doors—passed the living quarters of the *Vitamin's* senior staff. They dead-ended at a door marked "Bridge."

A security guard standing as stiff as a sentry said, "The captain told me you two were coming." He quickly wanded and patted down Damon. Albury was another story—he was armed. "I'm not sure if you're allowed inside with a firearm," the guard said, his hands shaking.

"I don't have time for this nonsense," Albury grunted. "Step aside."

The security guard permitted their entry, then asked Damon and the inspector to wait while he fetched the captain.

The *Vitamin's* bridge rivaled the luxury of a Fortune 500 company's board room. Floor-to-ceiling windows spanned its entire length. In the center stood a command center with an array of monitors, keyboards, manual controllers, and a pair of black-leather swivel chairs. One was occupied by a dark-skinned woman in her early forties who was wearing a badge that read "Second Officer." She wore a white, short-sleeve shirt with yellow epaulets and black slacks. Blue-gray carpet and a brown-leather loveseat and coffee table to one side of the command center gave the setting a serene feel.

Captain Harris appeared from a room behind the second officer and waved Damon and Albury toward him. After Harris, Albury, and Damon entered the conference room, the captain slid shut a gray door, closing the room off from the rest of the bridge.

Houston, Kitty, Miles, and Candice sat on one side of an oblong table. Amanda, Raymond, and Vicky—now accompanying the rest of the Drummillers—were positioned on the opposite side. Candice snuffled behind bedraggled black bangs and Raymond fidgeted in his seat. The others sat in stoic silence. The first officer and two stateroom attendants stood against the wall at one end of the room, despite open black-leather chairs. The captain joined his crew.

Inspector Albury stood at the head of the table. He directed Damon to a seat to his left and instructed everyone sitting at the table to introduce themselves.

"Thank you all for gathering here this morning," Albury started formally once the introductions were complete. "At approximately 6:55 this morning, a passenger taking the morning air at the back of the sixth deck saw a woman floating in the water, just a few feet from the ship's stern. Shortly thereafter, Mr. Lassard stopped on his jog to *rubberneck*. He identified the body as Mrs. Philippa Drummiller."

Damon flushed.

Albury turned to Miles. "Mr. Drummiller, I'll ask you to formally identify your wife after we're done here."

"Of course," Miles said quietly.

The inspector plowed ahead. "Because the death occurred in port, the Bahamas has sole jurisdiction over this matter. I have been informed by Captain Harris that there are six key cards on the ship that would open the door to Mrs. Drummiller's stateroom. Captain Harris has one, which I have seen. There was one in Philippa Drummiller's room—a SeaPass card—and another found on her person." Albury looked at the first officer, Eric Fraser, and asked, "Are you in possession of your master key?"

"I am," Fraser replied with nonchalance. He pulled a key card from his jacket pocket and held it in the air.

Albury scrawled a note on his pad, then directed his attention to Philippa's stateroom attendant and her supervisor. He asked them to produce their keys. They nodded in silent unison and each removed a key card from her apron.

"Thank you," Albury said. "That accounts for all six keys. You three may return to your duties."

Eva Ricaurte and her supervisor, Daniela Montalvo, shuffled out of the room quickly, Montalvo crossing herself repeatedly.

Damon made a mental note—like Captain Harris's, the keys Fraser and the housekeepers showed Albury looked just like the passengers' SeaPass cards, except theirs were black instead of light blue. Presumably their cards were programmed to open multiple doors, but Albury hadn't checked. If Fraser or either stateroom attendant had flashed a card that didn't open Philippa's door, then someone else could have a key to her room. In fact, Captain Harris's master card was the only one Inspector Albury or Damon had actually seen unlock Philippa's stateroom.

After Eric Fraser closed the sliding gray door shut behind him, Albury focused on Miles.

"Mr. Drummiller, when did you last see your wife alive?"

"When she went into her room last night," he responded. "At about twelve fifteen."

"And why were you not sharing a room with her?"

"I don't have to answer that," Miles said.

"It would be better if you did," Albury replied.

Miles stood abruptly. His cheeks reddened. "Is that some sort of accusation?"

Albury scratched at his notepad, but Damon noticed he wasn't actually writing anything down. The inspector gave Miles a hard look. "I'm not accusing you or anyone else in this room of anything. I just want a few facts."

"Oh, for heaven's sake, father," Candice said. "We all know you and Mother haven't slept in the same room for years." Her eyes were the only wet ones in the room.

Miles grunted and sat. "Candice's right," he said. "Philippa and I needed our space. It's not that we didn't spend time together. We did. Mr. Lassard and his mother saw us last night at one of the bars overlooking the promenade. But we slept separately."

"Did your wife know how to swim?" Albury asked.

Miles scowled and shook his head. "She never learned."

This time, Albury made a real note on his pad. The inspector looked around the table. "Was that common knowledge among the family? That she couldn't swim."

Everyone nodded. "Even Raymond and I knew, and we're technically not family," Vicky said. "We all e-mailed each other before coming on board to figure out which shore excursions we wanted to take. Philippa ruled out the snorkeling trips because she couldn't swim."

Inspector Albury turned his attention to Amanda. "Ms. Drummiller-Sweet, at any time since you boarded the ship, has the interior door adjoining your stateroom to Mrs. Drummiller's been opened?"

"Not that I know of," Amanda responded. "I never touched it."

"Me neither," Candice added.

Seconds of an awkward silence ticked by as Albury wrote notes on his pad. "Looks like we'll be missing our excursion today," Amanda ultimately said with a bitter edge, filling in the conversational gap.

Kitty shot her daughter a look.

"Provided the inspector permits it, has anyone made a decision about whether you all will be taking the body and leaving the ship here in Nassau?" Captain Harris asked.

All eyes at the table ping-ponged between Miles and Houston. After a moment, Houston said, "I recommend we finish our trip. As you explained to me a few minutes ago, Philippa can be embalmed in the ship's medical center."

Most of the family members nodded in agreement. Only Candice looked dismayed. "You're all going to go about your vacation while my mother is lying on ice?" she shouted.

"Your grandfather paid a lot of money for this vacation," Kitty said calmly.

"Even if the cruise staff screwed up and gave everyone rooms without balconies," Amanda muttered.

"Besides," Kitty added. "It will be much easier to handle transport from the United States than a foreign country."

"You people are sick," Candice moaned.

"Really, Candice?" Amanda sniped back. "When did you start caring so much about your mother? It hasn't even been twelve hours since you told me you hated her guts."

Candice stared at the table, mascara running down her cheeks. "Well, things have changed since then," she sputtered. "My mother drowned."

Damon rose from his chair and found a stack of napkins on a wooden ledge that ran the length of the room. He picked up a pair and handed them to Candice.

She dried her eyes and looked gratefully at Damon.

Inspector Albury resumed control, laying Philippa's suicide note—still enclosed in a plastic bag—on the table in front of himself, facing outward. The family members leaned toward it.

"What's that?" Houston asked from the far end of the table.

"It's a note I found in Mrs. Drummiller's nightstand," Albury said. "Mr. Lassard witnessed me finding it."

"What does it say?" Kitty asked, her voice rising.

The Bahamian turned the note around and read slowly. " 'The world has not been kind to me. I have a cheating husband, wicked daughter, and Houston Drummiller can rot in hell. I leave this life with a clear conscience. Philippa.' "

Silence filled the room for a solid ten seconds. "Well, that's that, I suppose," Vicky said, breaking the tension.

Albury looked at her intently. "I agree," he said, then examined each of the faces at the table. "Unless any of the cheating husband, wicked daughter, or Mr. Houston Drummiller has something to say."

More silence followed.

"Okay, then," Albury said. "I will be writing a brief report which I will ask Mr. Lassard to sign as a witness. It will state that between one o'clock last night, when the ship docked in Nassau, and approximately 6:55 this morning, when the body was first seen alongside the ship, Philippa Drummiller committed suicide. Mrs. Drummiller had pre-typed a suicide note, which she left in her stateroom. She locked the door to her room and went to a deserted part of the back side of the ship.

Given the ship's layout, it's likely she flung herself over the railing on deck six behind one of the two projection screens in the aquatics theater. A finding of suicide is supported by the fact that she had no external injuries. She couldn't swim so even if she changed her mind after hurling herself overboard, she would have perished. No one could hear screaming, if there was any, that far down, especially if the deck above was deserted."

"What about the staterooms that have balconies overlooking the aquatics theater?" Damon asked with incredulity. "Aren't you going to check to see if anyone saw her?"

Inspector Albury looked annoyed. "I believe the stage and projection screens would mask the railing at the back of the sixth deck from the vantage point of those rooms. But I will have my team check before we leave the ship."

Albury stood, offered flimsy condolences, and exited the room.

* * *

By the time Damon changed out of his jogging clothes, showered, and signed Albury's statement, it was nearly noon. He cruised by the ship's four swimming pools on the fifteenth deck in search of his mother. A five-piece steel drum band played background music.

Damon surveyed the pool scene—a healthy mix of ethnicities were represented. Plus, the passengers appeared thinner and less tattooed than the general population back home.

Damon found Lynne lying face up on a fully reclined lounge chair alongside a hot tub bearing a sign that read "adults only." She wore a modest one-piece suit and oversized sunglasses. Her feet were covered by a fluffy white towel.

"Where have you been?" Lynne asked as he sat on an empty lounger beside her. "Not that you have to tell me what you're doing at all hours."

Damon reached for the sunscreen his mother had set between the chairs and applied a palmful to the back of his neck, face, and forearms. "I went for a run but didn't make it more than a quarter of a mile." Damon filled in his mother on the morning's tragic events.

"My goodness. That's terrible," Lynne said when Damon finished. "I wonder if the captain will make an announcement?"

"And say what? There's a dead body literally chilling in the bowels of the ship?"

Lynne smacked his arm playfully. "Of course not. But I'm sure plenty of people saw the police presence—you said they cordoned off the boardwalk area. And you weren't the only passenger who saw Philippa's body in the water. Word will get around that someone died. And not of natural causes. People will whisper. They might start to wonder if there's a murderer on board."

Damon leaned in close to Lynne. A dab of white sunscreen dotted her forehead. He reached over and rubbed it into her skin. "Do you think Philippa could have been murdered?" Damon asked. "I'm sure not convinced she committed suicide."

Lynne, still on her back, flipped up her sunglasses and looked at her son. "Do I think Philippa was duped into going alone to an abandoned area of the ship in the middle of the night and then unceremoniously dumped over the railing? No, Damon, I don't. My point is simply that passengers on the *Vitamin* might *suspect* murder if the captain doesn't tell them it was a suicide. More likely though, they'll think it was an accident."

Damon started to protest, but Lynne raised a hand to stop him. "I know you helped Gerry Sloman solve two murders, and I think it's wonderful you'll be going through police academy training. And I'll admit that Philippa Drummiller struck me as a positively wretched woman. But that doesn't add up to murder."

"Maybe not, but I still don't think Inspector Albury conducted a thorough investigation, and he had every incentive to conclude it was a suicide. He told me he was trying to push down the homicide rate in the Bahamas." Damon sighed. "As soon as Albury found that typed note in Philippa's drawer, I could sense a change in his attitude—from apprehension to relief. He continued to act professionally, but he moved much more quickly. He wrapped up his entire investigation less than an hour after he found the letter."

"It does sound like a suicide letter," Lynne countered.

"Of course it *sounded* like one, but it was printed from a computer. Anyone could have typed it up before they came on board. Or for that matter, there are two computer centers with printers on the ship."

Chapter 5

Damon left his mother and ventured into the Galleon—an enormous buffet-style dining hall on the sixteenth deck. After receiving a quick squirt of Purell, he surveyed his options. The lunch-hour offerings seemed boundless—salad bars, grills, and deli stations competed with service counters filled with fresh fish, Caribbean delicacies, and Mediterranean dishes. Damon filled his plate high and then appraised a vast array of desserts.

"I keep losing weight, but it keeps finding me," a familiar voice said with a chuckle. Damon turned to see Amanda standing behind him with a full plate. Her smiled lingered.

"This place could give the best buffet in Las Vegas a run for its money," Damon said. "Would you care to join me at a table?"

"Sounds good. The rest of my family dispersed after that horrid meeting with the police inspector."

Damon followed Amanda as she weaved through tables occupied by passengers dressed in pool attire. But the seating area wasn't crowded—the *Vitamin* was in port and many of its passengers would be on land enjoying the best the Bahamas had to offer before the ship set sail in the late afternoon. Damon's eyes gravitated toward the sway of Amanda's hips. She was three or four years older than him, but she had an undeniable sensuality.

Amanda laid her plate on an open table for two.

"You have my sympathies," Damon said as they sat down.

"No big loss in my book," Amanda replied without a hint of emotion. "The woman was a gold digger, if you ask me."

Damon hadn't. "Is Miles extremely wealthy?"

"He's not Carlos Slim," she said, referencing the Mexican multibillionaire, "but our family's business has done very well."

"And you think Philippa married Miles for his money?"

"Actually," Amanda said with a smirk, "I think she married him to get to my father's money. Dad owns the bulk of the shares in Drummiller Box and Board. When he and my mother keel over, then Miles will be extremely wealthy."

"I suppose you will be, too." Damon regretted saying the words as soon as they escaped his lips. "Sorry," he said quickly. "I didn't mean…"

Amanda smiled coyly. "You didn't mean what?"

Embarrassed, Damon looked down at the teriyaki-glazed chicken wings on his plate. "Nothing," he murmured.

He sensed she was grinning at him. Damon looked up. Amanda's eyes had a glint of gold peeking through tobacco brown. "I'm curious," he said. "Why was Candice complaining about her mother last night to you? Did it have something to do with the *wickedness* Philippa mentioned in her letter?"

It was Amanda's turn to examine her food. Her plate was covered with a mix of fresh fruit and spinach salad. "It's personal."

"Sorry," Damon replied. "It's none of my business."

"Of course," Amanda said, tapping her fork against the table, "Candice doesn't care who knows. Philippa was the one who thought it was so scandalous."

Damon nibbled on a wing, waiting for her to continue.

"Candice got pregnant last year," Amanda said quietly. "Even though the father was an immature college boy who dropped her as soon as he found out, she wanted to keep the baby."

"But Philippa said no?" Damon ventured.

"Correct. Philippa didn't want a 'bastard grandchild.' Her words, not mine."

"And Candice capitulated?"

Amanda bit her lip. "Capitulated is a good word for it. She had the termination procedure. Absolutely appalling because Candice *wanted* to raise the baby. My niece may favor dressing in black and listening to music she calls deathrock, but she's a caring soul."

"Philippa must have put a lot of pressure on her."

"That's an understatement. She told Candice she would cut her off. Cold turkey. Candice would have to drop out of college and go work for minimum wage to support herself and the baby."

"Miles took Philippa's side?"

"I'm not sure, but he didn't back up his daughter. According to Candice, Miles told her not to 'make waves' in the family."

Damon wiped his mouth with a cloth napkin. "Why didn't Candice go to her grandfather? Surely, Houston could have supported her."

Amanda speared a broad leaf of spinach with her fork. "I don't know if she went to either of my parents for a lifeline. Father and Kitty would've considered having a child out of wedlock shameful." She paused to chew, then said, "They're very protective of the Drummiller family name, especially Kitty. It's funny, even I call my mother 'Kitty' these days."

Damon sipped lemonade and changed course. "How is your family handling Philippa's death?"

"I suppose they're dealing with it as expected. Candice is pretty upset, which makes sense—despite their differences, Philippa was her mother. Miles, on the other hand, is acting aloof. He and Philippa had been married for over twenty years, but they haven't been close for a long time."

"So why did they stay together?"

"My guess is Philippa wouldn't let go of the gravy train she was riding. Besides, Daddy would have frowned on a divorce. He's pretty conservative. And Miles is smart enough not to upset Daddy."

"And your mother?"

Amanda smiled and shook her head. "I suspect Kitty wouldn't have minded if Miles split with Philippa. Kitty was disappointed when Miles married her. I was fifteen at the time—old enough to overhear things at home and understand them." Amanda fanned herself with a napkin despite the cool, jet-pumped air flooding down from high ceiling vents.

"What kind of things?" Damon asked. He couldn't help prying.

"Kitty thought my brother married beneath us," she said with a laugh that Damon couldn't interpret. "It's an awful thing to say in this day and age, and Mother would never say as much in public—she's too much of a lady. But, given Daddy's wealth and their standing in the Raleigh-Durham community, Kitty wanted Miles to marry someone with a higher social status. Or at least a woman who came from money."

"Philippa didn't act like she came from a poor upbringing last night," Damon said.

"She certainly learned to lord over people with an oh-so-charming mix of self-righteousness and self-satisfaction." Amanda snickered. "And she wasn't poor but solidly middle class. Her parents drove American-made cars, drank beer from cans rather than bottles, and sent their kids to state colleges. That sort of thing. Her given name wasn't even Philippa."

A jolt of cold air pounded Damon's chest. He shivered reflexively.

Amanda continued, "Not long after she married Miles, she decided that Jennifer was too ordinary."

"Is Kitty still bitter, all these years later?" Damon asked.

"To be honest, I'm not sure," Amanda said. "My mother treated Philippa coolly but cordially." She bit into a perfectly shaped cube of tofu from her salad. After swallowing, she added, "I'm surprised Philippa killed herself. My sister-in-law acted with a lot of negativity, but she always directed it at others, never toward herself."

The more Damon heard about the inner workings of the Drummiller family, the more he convinced himself that Philippa's "suicide" hadn't come without uninvited assistance.

"It was interesting that Philippa only called out Miles, Daddy, and Candice in her note," Amanda said. "She didn't like me or Kitty any more than them."

"It didn't seem like she liked anyone," Damon replied. "Philippa's note said your brother was having an affair."

Amanda turned up the corners of her lips. "I doubt he was getting any physical satisfaction from Philippa. Her face puckered up like someone sucking on a lemon every time she looked at my brother," Amanda said, sidestepping Damon's veiled inquiry. "Philippa was much more attractive when she was younger. I suspect that's what hooked Miles in the first place. But the years haven't been good to her."

"And Miles would have gone for someone younger and better looking?"

"Not necessarily. He probably craved a woman's attention more than anything." Amanda reached across the table and touched Damon on the forearm. Then she added, "Men are pigs. If you want to find a committed man, look in a mental institution."

Damon laughed but sensed that Amanda was speaking from personal experience. Her last name was hyphenated, suggesting a husband had been in the picture at some point. But Candice was her onboard roommate, and Amanda wore no ring on her finger. Her marriage must have gone south. Damon didn't pursue the matter. Instead, he asked, "Do you know the source of Philippa's vitriol for Houston?"

"Why she wrote in her suicide note that Daddy should rot in hell? I have no idea." Amanda pulled back her hand and cast her eyes down to her plate. "To be honest, I'm surprised she wasn't sweeter to him. To get closer to his money."

Chapter 6

Damon passed the remainder of the afternoon on shore in Nassau with his mother. They ventured to the Atlantis resort and trekked through a stunning marine-life exhibit known simply as the Dig.

"Should I wear black to dinner tonight?" Damon asked Lynne after they returned to their stateroom.

"It's not a funeral," she replied. "It's just dinner."

"I know. But we have to sit with the Drummillers, and I imagine it's going to be a pretty somber affair."

"Maybe. But I suspect Jack will lighten the mood. That man is vivacious."

Damon shook his head. "I think litigious is more apt."

"He did have a mouthful of glass," Lynne said.

"Are you so sure he didn't put it there himself?"

* * *

Lynne offered quiet condolences as she and Damon sat down at their table in the Pelican Room. The Drummiller clan, less Philippa, was accounted for, as were Raymond and Vicky Carmichael. Stern expressions inhibited conversation, and an uncomfortable silence hovered over the table like a rain cloud.

"Why the glum faces folks?" Jack asked when he arrived at the table with Fava on his arm. She managed to look even more breathtaking than she had the previous evening. A silver cashmere sweater fitted snugly around her torso and a tight black skirt highlighted three inches of bronzed thighs.

Kitty looked at the pair of Texans. "You haven't heard?"

"Heard what?" Jack pulled out Fava's chair.

Houston placed a knotted hand over Kitty's. "My daughter-in-law, Philippa, passed away last night."

Fava clapped a hand over her mouth.

"That's awful," Jack said. "We've been off the ship since early this morning and hadn't heard." He thumped down into his seat. "You're at dinner, so does that mean you're staying aboard?"

"We are," Houston said. "It will be easier just to ride out the trip."

Candice cringed.

Fava looked from Houston, to Miles, to Candice. "I'm so very sorry," she said softly. "Would you like us to ask the headwaiter to seat us at another table so you can be alone?"

Damon hadn't considered that option. Kitty smiled graciously. "No, dear, that's not necessary," she said. "We want to try to enjoy the time we have on board. But if you're uncomfortable, we wouldn't be offended if you'd prefer to sit elsewhere."

"Uncomfortable, ha!" Jack said. "I've never been uncomfortable for a day in my life."

Damon noticed Fava looked anxious, nibbling on a fingernail. He wondered if it was solely due to her placement with the Drummillers or if she was less than enchanted with her cruising companion.

The level of uneasiness at the table jumped a notch when the waiters—Niels and Kristjan—approached. Jack had been very curt with them after the glass incident the previous evening.

Niels relayed the night's specials in a professional tone. Kristjan didn't speak. He went from diner to diner and jotted down their orders. Then the two retreated to the kitchen.

"So, Jack, what did you and Fava do in Nassau today?" Lynne asked, breaking the tension.

"Fava went swimming with the dolphins, right, darling?" Jack said.

"It was one of the most memorable things I've ever done," Fava answered with enthusiasm. "I rubbed their tummies and held a hula hoop for them to jump through."

"You didn't go?" Lynne asked Jack.

"Unfortunately not," Jack said. "I was on the phone with my lawyer for most of the day. I'm filing a suit against the company that owns this cruise line. Emotional distress and all." He sipped light brown liquid from a tumbler he'd brought to the table.

He doesn't look too distressed to me, Damon thought.

"You're distressed?" Candice asked, obviously sharing Damon's opinion. "Aren't you just taking advantage of an unfortunate accident?"

Jack turned to face the newly minted twenty-one-year-old. "It's all about posturing, my dear girl. Emotional anguish is just one arrow in my lawyer's quiver. He's demanding $3 million in damages."

"Three million?" Candice snapped. The muscles in her face visibly tensed.

"It's just a tactic," Jack said smoothly. "When we ask for that much, the fleet's owners will file a claim with their insurance company. The insurer won't risk going court, so they'll offer to settle privately. My lawyer's best estimate is I'll get about a tenth of the three million. So the cruise line pays an insurance deductible of twenty thousand or so to get off the hook. I get three-hundred large. I pass along ten percent to my lawyer. Everyone's happy."

Everyone except the insurance company, Damon thought. Jack seemed to know exactly how the scenario would run its course. Either his attorney had explained it very comprehensively or Jack had played this game before.

"Well, after biting into that glass last night, I'm thankful you're all right, Mr. Jackman," Vicky said. "One death at our table this week is plenty." She began to laugh but quickly closed her mouth when no one joined her.

"Did your wife die peacefully?" Fava asked Miles.

Miles snorted. "No. She didn't have enough grace to die in her sleep. She threw herself off the deck of the ship. May as well have been a strung-out teenager jumping off of the Brooklyn Bridge."

"Father, you have no compassion for anyone," Candice said to Miles. "All you care about is your company."

"Watch your tone, young lady," Miles retorted. "And that's not true. I *do* care about people."

Damon caught Miles and Vicky exchanging an intimate glance. And then it hit him—Vicky was the other woman in Miles's life. A middle-aged vamp who married Houston's godson but snuck out with his flesh-and-blood offspring. She'd probably been in Miles's stateroom when Damon arrived with Captain Harris and Inspector Albury that morning.

Kristjan brought an array of soups and salads to the table, and the gathering grew quiet as the diners focused on their starters.

Damon mentally arranged what he knew so far. Assuming Miles and Vicky were an item, each would have a motive to kill Philippa. Vicky's was twofold—she could potentially land both Miles and his money. Of course, she'd have to get rid of her husband first. For Miles, eliminating his wife would ease the path to deepening an ongoing affair with Vicky. Then again, by default a surviving husband was a prime suspect in almost any murder investigation, at least on television. Miles could have any number of reasons to kill Philippa.

Another obvious suspect was Candice. Philippa had forced her daughter to terminate her pregnancy. That wouldn't be something any woman could easily forgive. But Candice's reaction to Philippa's death appeared heart-wrenching—at least compared to the other Drummillers, none of whom had shed a single tear in Damon's presence. Had Candice feigned grief to throw off anyone who might become suspicious? Then again, Candice *was* Philippa's daughter. No other family member on the ship was related to Philippa by blood.

Damon picked at his Caesar salad. The other bit of gossip Damon had gleaned was that Kitty hadn't approved of Miles's marriage. The heavyset matron viewed Philippa as beneath the Drummiller family. But if Kitty's solution to an unfavorable marriage was to do away with her daughter-in-law, why wait more than twenty years?

As far as Damon knew, the only other people on board who knew Philippa were her father-in-law, Houston; sister-in-law, Amanda; and Raymond Carmichael. Based on his impression of Amanda, Damon suspected that if she had a grievance with Philippa, she would have hashed it out with her in the open, rather than resort to violence in the small hours of the night.

Damon didn't have a good sense of the thin-lipped Raymond. He'd have to learn more.

Houston was the last of the bunch Damon considered. Philippa clearly had animosity toward the man—her suicide note said that Houston could "rot in hell."

Damon mentally checked himself. If Philippa had been murdered, she hadn't written the note. If every point in the note was true, the killer had to know Miles was unfaithful, Candice had gotten herself pregnant—assuming that was the *wickedness* referred to in the note—and that Philippa disdained Houston. But, on the other hand, there was nothing to stop the murderer from making up a story or two to cast suspicion on a fellow family member in case the suicide ruse was debunked. Would the killer include his or her own name in the note? He decided that was a question for someone who had a better grasp of psychology than he.

As an entrée of swordfish over saffron rice was laid in front of him, another thought struck Damon. Inspector Albury had officially ruled Philippa's death a suicide. Without the police investigating, if Philippa had been murdered, the killer might let down his or her guard, just a hair. As long as Damon didn't let on that he was rooting around for clues related to Philippa's death, he might be able to gather information without raising suspicion. He decided to tackle Raymond, albeit softly.

"Raymond, what do you do for a living?" Damon asked.

Raymond leveled a brief glare in Miles's direction, then turned his attention to Damon. "I'm the foreman at a plastics plant outside of Wilmington, Delaware. Injection molding. We make everything from grommets to medical syringes."

"Sounds like an interesting line of work," Damon said out of courtesy.

"Not really," Raymond replied. "I just fix the machines when they break and make sure we get the right amount of product out the door."

"How long have you been there?" Lynne asked him.

"About ten years."

"He started in the cardboard business," Vicky added. "But he couldn't cut it like Houston or Miles."

Raymond gave his wife a sideways stare but kept his mouth shut.

Candice stood up. "I'm skipping dessert. If you'll excuse me, I'll be on my way."

"Candice, dear, tonight's your birthday," Kitty said. "I thought we could order some cake and sing."

"Thank you, grandmother, but I'm going to pass. And I forgot to say thank you for the flowers you had delivered to my room last night."

Kitty nodded.

"Where are you going?" Miles injected sternly.

Candice turned to face her father. "Not that I have to answer to you, but I'm going to the Irish pub. I met one of the bartenders last night, and I'm going to hang out with him while he pours drinks for the snobs on board this ship. Then I'll probably cry myself to sleep," she said maudlinly. "It hasn't even been twenty-four hours since Mother died."

Chapter 7

An hour and a quarter later, Damon planted himself in a black-and-white, houndstooth chair at a ten-dollar blackjack table, sandwiched between an overweight investment banker and a chain smoker sporting a bolo tie. The smoke bothered Damon, but not enough to give up his seat. Damon wasn't much of a gambler but had learned to hold his own in Macau on a series of junkets sponsored by Kushiro Chewing Gum—the company that had paid Damon and his Japanese teammate to hawk their products.

The decibel level in the casino was high—slot machine sirens competed with alcohol-infused laughter. Blood-red wallpaper with a black-and-yellow sunburst motif clashed with a crimson carpet patterned with black clubs, spades, hearts, and diamonds.

Damon had given himself a modest limit and, after forty-five minutes of play, was up fifty dollars. He sensed a presence behind him and smelled a fragrance redolent of vanilla. His blackjack hand busted, and Damon peeked back over his shoulder. Fava looked down on him with her clear blue eyes.

"Keep playing," she said with a sugary southern accent and rested a hand on Damon's shoulder. A ripple of excitement coursed through his veins. Damon had reasonable luck with the fairer sex, but it still amazed him when an extremely attractive woman expressed interest.

He played for another ten minutes but couldn't concentrate and started to make mistakes. The chain smoker leaned in close and whispered into Damon's ear, "What the hell are you doing, buddy? Get your sorry tail up and buy that woman a drink."

Damon took the man's advice and stood.

To Fava, he said, "I'm losing my shirt here. Any interest in a nightcap?"

"Sounds good," she replied. "But can we go somewhere more private? Maybe the Lion's Crown?"

The pair made their way in a glass elevator to the seventeenth deck—the uppermost level of the ship. The Lion's Crown was an oval-shaped perch with windows looking down over the pool area. A staffer pointed Damon and Fava to the requisite hand sanitizer. Fava winced as she rubbed the cool gel between her fingers. Low lights and a smooth-jazz quartet engendered a romantic atmosphere. Couples engaged in hushed conversations at tables for two. Damon and Fava found a spot in a corner away from the band. They ordered drinks from a discreet waiter.

"How are you?" Damon asked gently. "It's been an eventful two days."

"It certainly has been," Fava said. "I can't imagine life becoming so difficult that committing suicide was my only option." She paused. "Damon, you seem very level-headed. I was hoping I could speak with you about Jack."

The waiter returned with their drinks—Guinness for Damon and a pomegranate margarita for Fava.

"Go ahead," Damon said after the waiter departed.

"I don't think I trust Jack anymore." Fava's tone was one of regret.

"Have you been dating long?"

"About three months. I met Jack at a political fundraiser. He was a donor, and I was working as a greeter. That's probably too generous of a term—I was paid eye candy." She smiled sadly. "I was studying to be a nurse but had to drop out when my father passed away a couple of years ago. My mother has PTS after serving in the Gulf War. She's not able to work so I have to support her."

"I'm so sorry." Damon could feel his heart thudding.

"It's okay." Fava rewarded his concern by looking deeply into Damon's eyes. "It just meant working six days a week at a bakery and taking odd jobs when I could get them to cash in on my looks."

"I'm surprised you aren't modeling."

"You're very charming, Damon Lassard," she said and gave him an impish wink. "Unfortunately, modeling requires too much travel, and I have to care for my mother. My brother finally graduated from high school and works now, but the timing of his shifts can be erratic. It took a tremendous amount of coordination for me to get away for this cruise. Anyway, I decided that the paltry wage I was making at the bakery and money from working events sporadically wasn't enough. So I scaled back to part-time at the bakery, put my dignity aside, and went for a cash cow."

"Meaning Jack?"

She nodded. "A lot of the girls on the Dallas circuit do it."

"The circuit?"

"Girls who take jobs as nightclub hostesses, auto-show models, things like that. Basically, dead-end posts where a girl can get by on her looks alone. She'll find a wealthy and lonely man and give him some attention. Usually, it's an older guy who's divorced or a widower. It gets his juices flowing to have a much younger woman on his arm."

Damon sipped his beer.

"It's degrading," Fava continued. "But after a few dates, the gentleman will usually start buying a girl gifts. Anything from perfume to jewelry. The goal is to find a man who'll pay your rent and maybe even your car payments. The ultimate score is a spending allowance."

"A spending allowance?" Damon repeated.

"A few thousand dollars a month. The unwritten rule is that when a man gives you an allowance, you quit your job. That way, you can be available whenever he calls at a moment's notice." Fava stirred her margarita.

"Does Jack give you an allowance?"

"No, but he's pretty generous. Jack pays most of my bills and slips me a couple of hundreds every time I see him, which is two or three times a week. It adds up."

"He must be pretty wealthy," Damon observed.

Fava leaned forward across the table. "That's what I wanted to talk to you about," she whispered. "I think he's lying about his business interests. He tells everyone he's an importer. He says he has suppliers all over the world and distribution channels throughout the United States. But I don't believe it."

Damon's ears prickled with excitement. "Why's that?"

Fava moistened her lips. "First of all, I never see him doing any real work. Like I said, I'm only with him a few times a week, but he never receives any business calls. Also, I may have ... um ... gone through the drawers in his office once while he was taking a nap." She cast her eyes toward her drink. "I didn't find anything related to the import trade. It's possible he keeps everything on his computer, but you'd think I'd find some trace of his transactions."

"So if he's not an importer," Damon said, playing along, "how do you think he came into his money?"

Fava looked up at Damon. "I think he files bogus lawsuits."

"Me too!" He quickly looked to either side of the table. No one was paying attention to them. He lowered his voice and added, "He seemed to know way too well how to handle the situation last night, from taking pictures to getting witness statements."

"Exactly," Fava whispered. "And in less than twenty-four hours, he and his lawyer already have a game plan. He's already counting his money."

"We could look him up online and see if he's been involved in lawsuits before," Damon suggested.

"I did that this afternoon. After swimming with the dolphins, I told Jack I was going to a day spa. But I went to an Internet café instead."

"And?" Damon asked.

Fava started to speak, then paused as their waiter approached and wordlessly set a complimentary plate of chocolate-chip cookies on the table.

"I came up empty," Fava said when the waiter was out of earshot. "I think he threatens to file lawsuits and then he and his attorney settle before going to court. That way, there's no public record."

"So if the cruise line's lawyers look up Jack before offering to settle," Damon started.

"He'd look as clean as a whistle," Fava said, finishing his sentence.

"Does he have a website for his import business?"

"Yes, but it's completely bare bones—a single page with some generic pictures and an e-mail address."

"A site he could make by himself in fifteen minutes," Damon commented.

Fava tugged on a strand of silky brown hair and pressed her top teeth into her lower lip. "Damon, I feel very comfortable with you," she said after a moment. "There's something that happened yesterday before dinner."

Damon leaned forward. "What happened?"

She took a deep breath, then asked: "Did someone hand you and your mother flutes of champagne when you boarded the ship yesterday?"

"Yes. I think the crew passed them out to everyone."

"That's what I thought. We got them, too. After we went to our stateroom, I distinctly remember setting both of our empty flutes on the nightstand. Then we went off to explore the ship."

Damon noticed Fava's teeth as she spoke. They were perfectly straight with no hint of yellow.

"When we came back into the room to dress for dinner last night," Fava continued, "the flutes were just where I left them. I took a shower while Jack unpacked his clothes. When I came out of the bathroom, both champagne glasses were gone."

"Did you hear anything?" Damon asked.

"Like breaking glass? No. I didn't say anything to Jack about the missing flutes at the time because it didn't seem important. But when Jack pulled the sliver of glass from his mouth at dinner and found another one in his potatoes, it made me think. The shards looked thin, like glass from a champagne flute."

"Did you confront him?"

"I didn't overtly accuse him of anything, but when we returned to our room after dinner last night, I asked him if he knew what happened to the champagne glasses that had been on the nightstand. At first he said the stateroom attendant must have taken them when she turned down our bed for the night. But I told Jack they'd disappeared while I was in the shower. He couldn't mask his guilt—his face looked like a ten-year-old's, caught with stolen candy in his pocket. After a second, he recovered and said, 'My mistake, I had forgotten. While you were in the shower, I set them in the hall for the crew to clear.'"

"You don't believe him?" Damon asked. He longed to reach across the table and take Fava's hands in his but restrained himself.

"I don't," she said. "How could he forget that he set the glasses in the hall—it was only a few hours earlier. Plus, I didn't hear him open the door while I was in the shower."

"Would you have?" Damon asked. "You said you didn't hear glass breaking, either."

"Maybe not," Fava allowed. "Between the running water and the confined shower space, it would be pretty difficult to hear anything outside of the bathroom." She sipped her drink, then said, "Not hearing a champagne flute break doesn't mean anything. Jack could have put one inside of a towel or a T-shirt to dampen the noise."

"Good point. And after breaking the glass, all he had to do was slip a few shards into his pants pockets to use at dinner. But I doubt he'd risk putting a broken flute in the hallway. One of the housekeepers might remember if the cruise line's lawyer started asking questions."

"That's exactly what I've been thinking," Fava said. "I bet the stem of a broken champagne glass is still in our stateroom. And an intact one, too, for that matter."

"Those glasses disappeared from your nightstand more than twenty-four hours ago," Damon countered. "Surely, Jack's disposed of them. For all we know, he could be dumping the remnants right now."

"I don't think so." Fava reached for her margarita, then changed her mind and let her fingers dance across the table to the back of Damon's hand. She grazed it lightly with perfectly shaped nails. "He's playing in a Texas Hold'em tournament in the casino's poker room. It's a two-hour commitment—even if you lose all of your chips, you can buy back in. And he hasn't been alone in our room since last night."

"Are you sure?" Damon asked, relishing the touch of Fava's fingertips.

She retracted her hand slowly. "After dinner yesterday, we spent the rest of the evening in our room together. I was tending to the cut in his mouth, which wasn't too deep. Then after breakfast this morning, we got off of the ship and spent the whole day on shore in Nassau. We reboarded, changed, went to dinner, saw the ice-skating show, and now he's playing in the poker tournament."

"But you were swimming with the dolphins and then went to an Internet café without Jack," Damon said. "He could have gone back on board while you were apart."

"Nope," Fava replied quickly. "I had his SeaPass card. As you know, you can't reboard the ship without it."

Damon grinned. "That was good thinking."

"A happy accident. Before I realized Jack wouldn't be joining me on the dolphin excursion, I tucked a few of his things into my purse—sunglasses, sunscreen, and his SeaPass card. I could tell Jack was upset when we met up to reboard this afternoon. The first thing he asked me was whether I had his card. He pretended to be concerned that he'd lost it, but I think he'd planned to go back on board while we were apart."

"Did you take a shower tonight, before dinner?" Damon asked. "Jack could have slipped out of the room and tossed the broken stem and any remaining shards down a trash chute. Or, if your room has a balcony, he could have thrown the pieces overboard."

Fava shook her head. "I didn't need to shower in the room today. The marine park had full facilities so I took one there after swimming with the dolphins."

"How about last night, while you were sleeping?"

"I'm a very light sleeper. I'm sure I would have heard him."

Damon took a sip of Guinness. "So you think there's a broken champagne flute in your stateroom right now?"

"I do. Jack suggested I go to breakfast by myself tomorrow morning. He said he needed to get some work done in the room. I don't buy it—I think he's planning to dispose of the broken champagne flute. I'd like to tell ship security or the headwaiter from the Pelican Room about my suspicions. If I could only find the broken glass, I'd know for sure it was the right thing to do."

"We could look for it now," Damon suggested.

"Would you help me do that?" Fava asked, latching on to the idea. "I couldn't bear to look by myself."

"I'd love to help." Damon was excited to scratch his sleuthing itch. "Why don't you check in on Jack first, to make sure he's still in the poker room. Then we'll search your room. I met the *Vitamin's* captain this morning. If we find a broken flute, we'll take it straight to Captain Harris."

"Thanks, Damon," Fava said. "I think I need to call it quits with Jack. He's more charismatic and better looking than most of the older gentlemen I've run across, but I can't stomach spending so much time with someone I'm not interested in. Especially if he's a hustler." Tears pooled in her eyes. She dabbed them quickly with a napkin and rose. Outdoor flood lights streaming into the glass-fronted lounge accentuated her figure.

They made their way back down to the casino, and Fava ducked into the poker room—a football-shaped space surrounded by walls covered in a burgundy, suede-like fabric stitched into a diamond pattern. While Damon waited in the doorway, Fava confirmed that

Jack was still playing cards; he'd be occupied for another forty minutes.

* * *

For the second time that day, Damon found himself involved in a stateroom search. Only this time, he was allowed to participate. He and Fava carefully picked through Jack's luggage and toiletries, and a nightstand identical to the one that had borne fruit for Inspector Albury in Philippa's room.

They struck out until Damon opened a dresser drawer where Jack had neatly folded his shorts and undergarments. A nip of a blue hand towel peeked out from beneath a stack of the man's Jockey shorts. Damon motioned Fava to his side.

He removed Jack's clothing and set it on the carpet. Then Damon carefully unwrapped the towel. To his surprise and disappointment, he found two fully intact champagne flutes etched with the *Vitamin's* logo.

"I don't understand," Fava said looking over his shoulder. "He lied to me about putting the glasses in the hall, but he didn't break either one?"

As Damon lifted out one of the flutes to inspect it, he saw a yellow sticky note attached to the towel. It read: "*Reminder of first trip with Fava. Give on one-year anniversary.*" Damon pointed at the note, and Fava peered inside the drawer.

"A keepsake?" she said and paused. "That's actually sort of sweet."

Damon felt a burning sensation in the pit of his stomach. He'd been wrong about Jack. Maybe his instincts for detection weren't as good as he thought they were. He reassembled the towel-wrapped flutes and replaced Jack's clothing in the drawer.

"I suppose that's why Jack told me he put the glasses in the hall," Fava said. "So he could surprise me nine months from now. Not that I'm likely be with him."

"You're still going to drop him?" Damon asked with a hint of optimism creeping into his voice.

She patted his arm but didn't respond directly. "Come on," she said, "let's get out of here."

Chapter 8

"Does the name Pavlov ring a bell?" Lynne said.

"What are you talking about?" Damon asked. They were lying awake in their stateroom at a little past midnight, Lynne in the bed and Damon on the pull-out sofa. He had just finished bringing her up to speed on his excursion with Fava.

"What I mean," Lynne said, "is that Fava played you like a fiddle. I know because, in a way, I orchestrated it."

Damon sat up and flipped on a wall sconce.

"Shut that off," Lynne hissed. "I was trying to help you."

"Okay, mother. Please start making some sense." He turned the light off but remained sitting.

"Just after dinner tonight I ran into Jack."

"At the ice show?"

"No. I was in one of the shops on the promenade looking at swimsuits when Jack strolled in behind me."

Damon's spirits sank. Had Fava lied about being with Jack at the ice show after dinner?

"I told him you thought he put the shards of glass in his mashed potatoes," Lynne said.

"What?" Damon shouted. He turned the light back on. "Are you crazy?"

"No," she said calmly. "I wanted to flush him out to see what he'd do."

Damon blinked several times, adjusting his eyes to the light, then stared at Lynne. "This isn't a movie."

"I know, but I couldn't think of any other way to find out if he's a con man."

"Mother, half an hour before we went to the Pelican Room tonight you were singing his praises."

Lynne hid her face under a pillow. "I changed my mind about Jack during dinner." Her voice was muffled. "When he started talking so confidently about how he'd wind up hundreds of thousands of dollars richer, I decided you were right. He's operating too smoothly."

Damon shook his head in frustration. "So you told him I was suspicious of him?"

"The word I used was wary, but yes. Of course, I told Jack I disagreed with you, and I was certain that a negligent kitchen staffer was responsible for the glass."

"So you stay innocent, and I'm the distrustful one. Thanks a lot."

Lynne pulled the pillow from her face. "But you didn't believe him, did you? And look at what happened as a result of my little ploy."

Damon made a circling gesture with his hand, prompting Lynne to explain.

"Isn't it obvious? Jack and Fava set you up to get you to back off."

It was Damon's turn to bury his head under a pillow. "I'm listening."

"I wasn't sure if Fava was in on the scheme. But now it's evident that she's been involved from the start. Less than two hours after I raised your suspicions with Jack, Fava was by your side concocting a scheme to hunt for a broken champagne flute she knew you wouldn't find."

Damon popped his head back up. "It was *my* idea to search their room."

"Rubbish—that's what she made you *think*. Damon, I love you, but you can be a bit naïve when a beautiful woman's involved."

Damon grunted, knowing she was right.

"I have no doubt Jack and Fava planned it," Lynne said. "They could have gone to any bar on the ship and ordered champagne. You can carry glasses anywhere on board. So they drained two flutes and hid them inside a towel in Jack's underwear drawer. Then Jack went to play poker and Fava devised a clever story. You fell right in line. By the time you walked out of Jack and Fava's stateroom, you had changed your mind about Jack's guilt, right?"

"I had," Damon admitted. "But why manufacture such an elaborate stunt? I didn't have any concrete evidence against them."

"Because I told Jack that you have a history of solving crimes," Lynne said. "I wouldn't be surprised if he or Fava went to one of the computer centers and found the newspaper stories that highlight your crime-solving skills. After reading those, they may have felt compelled to take action."

As the information sank in, Damon realized his mother was probably right.

"Think about it," Lynne continued. "If Fava suspected Jack of wrongdoing, why enlist your help in searching their room?"

"She was too scared to do it herself," Damon said unconvincingly.

"I don't think so."

Damon inhaled deeply. His initial gut reaction to Jack had likely been correct. That was a relief. But he resigned himself to the fact that Fava had seduced him for reasons completely unrelated to his desirability.

Damon flicked off the light, tucked his head back under his pillow, and tried to put the day behind him.

* * *

Tuesday, January 14

Sea days were bustling on board the *Vitamin*. The pools and buffet were packed by nine thirty in the morning. The ship's entertainment staff would hold events as varied as cupcake decorating, bingo, and flash-mob dance classes to keep passengers busy as they slowly cruised toward Saint Thomas—the *Vitamin's* destination for the following day.

Damon and Lynne decided to skip breakfast in the Galleon and strode side by side into the park on the eighth deck. The air smelled damp, and small puddles dotted a curved sidewalk cutting through the park's foliage. A groundskeeper was giving a cluster of elderly passengers a tour of the gardens. Three high-end restaurants lined one edge of the park—evening dining was available at an additional cost for passengers seeking an alternative to the Pelican Room or its counterparts. On the opposite side, tucked between an art gallery and a luxury leather shop, stood the quaint and aptly named Park Café.

Damon and Lynne stepped inside and reviewed the breakfast offerings. Damon skipped a lengthy line at the design-your-own-bagel bar and opted for a croissant, Greek yogurt, and a steaming mug of coffee. Lynne chose mixed fruit and muesli.

They sat at a small stone-topped table in front of the café. Morning sun warmed Damon's forehead in front of his receding hairline.

Ten minutes into breakfast, Houston and Kitty approached their table with filled plates.

"May we join you?" Kitty asked. She wore a loose off-the-rack cotton dress that helped to mask her weight but contrasted sharply with her glistening ruby necklace.

Lynne nodded, and Damon retrieved a pair of empty chairs from a nearby table.

"How are you holding up?" Lynne asked.

"We're doing all right," Kitty replied. "Thank you for asking."

"It must be nice for Miles and Candice to have their family around them for support," Damon said.

"In theory, it would be," Houston said. "But I don't know how much grieving my son is doing. There wasn't a lot of love lost between Miles and Philippa. Heck, he spends more time with Vicky."

Damon raised his eyebrows, but Lynne kicked him below the table before he could speak.

Houston noticed Damon's interest and added, "Oh, Miles just likes to get under Raymond's skin. Those two aren't exactly the best of friends."

Damon picked at his yogurt.

"Houston, Lynne and Damon don't want to hear about our family's squabbles," Kitty said.

Yes I do, Damon wanted to shout.

Lynne turned to face Houston. "If you need to get something off of your mind to strangers, it's okay," she said.

Damon was surprised by his mother's interest. She was one of the few residents of their Hollydale community not typically prone to gossip. Then again, she had goaded Jack Jackman into taking action the previous evening.

Houston blew air from his bearded cheeks. "It was just a business disagreement, nothing more," he said. "Miles and Raymond both started with our company twenty years ago. My partner, Zachary Bristol, was still with me at the time. We trained the boys from the ground up, on everything from the mundane to the sophisticated—from operating the machinery to working with our financiers and attorneys. Miles took to the business right off the bat. Raymond had more trouble. But he was my godson so I pushed him along."

Houston paused to stuff his mouth with a poppy-seed bagel piled high with lox and red onions, then swallowed.

"I bought Zach's share of the business five years after the boys started," Houston continued. "He wanted to retire early. Me on the other hand, I had my mind set on expansion. A few years later, I decided the time was right to give Miles and Raymond the chance to have some skin in the game. I agreed to pass along ten percent of the company to the boys, based on merit. So I held a little contest."

Riveted, Damon pushed his plate aside.

"I gave them six months to go out and expand operations," Houston said. "I told them I'd divvy up the ten percent in proportion to the amount of new business they brought in. Miles started pitching to companies up and down the East Coast. Raymond focused on the city where he grew up, Wilmington, Delaware. After the first five months, Miles had done remarkably well—he'd landed six new clients. They were all midsized but rock solid. Raymond had yet to sign on anyone, but he had a whopper on the line: a national grocery chain. That account alone was worth three times as much as the ones Miles had lined up, combined. The problem was, Raymond couldn't close the deal."

Kitty picked a small piece of salmon from Houston's beard and set it on the edge of her plate.

"Thank you, dear," Houston said. He turned his attention back to Lynne. "At the end of the day, Raymond was stuck. So Miles came in and finished the job."

"How'd he pull that off?" Lynne asked. "If he and Raymond were both selling Drummiller boxes."

"Miles was a better salesman. The boy could sell water to a whale!" Houston chortled. "Honestly, Miles knew the products better, and he was light years ahead of Raymond when it came to discussing the company's infrastructure and financial stability. Miles carried the Drummiller name, too."

"Did Miles receive the whole ten percent?" Damon asked.

"Yep. Fair's fair. Raymond left the company soon thereafter. It was the right move for all of us—he wasn't cut out for a senior-level position, and we all knew it."

"I assume you'll retire at some point and Miles will take over," Lynne said.

"Absolutely. Miles is ready to take the reins. I'm planning to retire in about a year so Kitty and I can travel the world." Houston smoothed his beard with his hands.

"I think it's just lovely that you're passing the family business to your son," Lynne said.

"Houston's a wonderful father," Kitty chimed in. "He put his ninety percent of the company in a trust for Miles and Amanda, too."

Houston smiled at his wife. "That way we never have to worry about them after Kitty and I croak."

"I am not planning to *croak*, Houston." Kitty slapped him lightly on the wrist.

"It's very thoughtful that you've made such provisions for your family," Lynne said.

Damon wondered whether Raymond, who apparently didn't have any shares in Drummiller Box and Board earmarked for him, would consider his godfather so thoughtful.

"Just trying to do right for my family," Houston said, then glanced down at his watch. "If you'll all excuse me, I have somewhere to be." He rose, kissed Kitty's cheek, and left the table.

"He's meeting with a private trainer in the fitness center," Kitty whispered as her husband walked out of the park.

After another ten minutes of light conversation, Kitty set off to partake in a tour of the ship's artwork, and Lynne headed up to the pool deck. Damon lingered behind. He'd spotted Niels, the waiter from the Pelican Room, serving pastries inside the café, and he wanted to ask him some questions.

* * *

Fifteen minutes later, Niels's shift ended, and he came outside to Damon's table.

"You wanted to speak with me, Mr. Lassard?" Niels began to wipe down the table with a wet cloth.

"Please call me Damon. Will you join me for a cup of coffee?"

"Unfortunately, no. We're not supposed to interact with passengers except on a professional level." He held up the wash rag by way of explanation.

"Oh, okay. I was surprised to see you working in the café."

Niels sighed. "You and me both. With the norovirus outbreak last week, the whole crew has to work extra shifts in the spots that are usually self-service. Not to mention standing over those Purell dispensers like totalitarian germaphobes."

Damon noticed that Niels looked more comfortable than he did in the Pelican Room—probably due to his comparatively casual attire. "I was hoping to speak with you about the glass that Jack Jackman bit into the other night," Damon said.

Niels looked up, his hand continuing to wipe the table in a circular pattern. "Go on," he said cautiously.

"I'm not convinced that Mr. Jackman's being honest. Do you know if anyone from the kitchen staff found any broken glass near the potatoes?"

"Not that I'm aware of." Niels quickly looked from side to side, as if he was afraid of being overheard. "My girlfriend Roberta is a supervisor in the galley that prepares food for the Pelican Room and its two counterparts. She told me the girl who was prepping potatoes that night swears she didn't break a glass. Of course, that doesn't mean much. Why would she admit it?"

"Can I speak with her?" Damon asked.

"No way. Food-prep personnel aren't allowed in the passenger areas of the ship."

"Not even this week while the crew is doling out food and hand sanitizer?"

"Good point. But I don't know where or when she might be stationed."

Damon sighed, thinking: *You could just ask her.* Instead, he extended the truth. "Back in the States, I'm a private investigator, and I'm training to be a police detective. I want to help the ship because I think Jack Jackman's a scoundrel. Would it be possible for you to take me into the galley that serves the Pelican Room?"

Niels scrubbed hard on the spotless table. After thirty seconds, he said, "All right. I heard that Ricki, the girl who was on potato duty, might get fired. If there's any chance to save her job, I can't just stand by." He looked up at Damon. "There's one condition: If anyone asks, you already *are* a police detective and you forced me to take you into the crew-only area."

"Done," Damon replied without hesitation.

Chapter 9

The enormous galley servicing the *Vitamin's* formal dining rooms was a testament to cleanliness. Fluorescent lights shone down on half an acre of stainless-steel appliances and gleaming countertops. Rows of dishwashing machines behind mesh caging hummed like finely tuned engines. Computer screens mounted on the walls displayed a meal ordering-and-tracking system.

Chefs in crisp white coats with cuffed sleeves and paper hats went about their business with quiet efficiency as Damon and Niels passed through areas dedicated to baking, stews, and soups. A chef with a yellow necktie stirred a brown concoction, smelling of beef stroganoff, with a metal oar in a stainless-steel vat the size of a bathtub. Across from him, a woman wearing a blue necktie added carrots to a soup drum with a ladle that could hold a basketball.

"The chefs in yellow neckties are new," Niels explained. "It's their first year on a ship. Supervisors who have been on staff for at least five years get a red necktie. Everyone else wears a blue one. Except the executive chef and sous-chef. They don't wear one at all."

"Are they all preparing for dinner tonight?" Damon asked.

"The majority. We do offer a sit-down lunch service but don't get many takers. Most passengers don't want to change out of their bathing suits and shorts in the middle of the day to put on the dress pants and nice shirts required in the formal dining rooms."

They approached an open room dominated by four massive stainless-steel tables, each covered by row upon row of shrimp cocktails in shell-shaped silver cups. A gathering of six chefs stood around the tables assembling the appetizers.

As Niels stopped in front of the nearest table, a thought crashed into Damon's head. Had Jack and Fava worked with a crew member? No, he reasoned, the staff served thousands of entrées each night in the formal dining rooms—they couldn't possibly earmark a particular plate for a particular passenger. Unless a food preparer was working with a server. *Too many people*, Damon thought; Jack and Fava would have to be in cahoots with both a chef and a waiter. Then again, Niels had said he *was* dating one of the chefs.

"Damon, this is my girlfriend, Roberta." Niels gestured toward a tall woman with large dark eyes and other facial features that reminded Damon of a chipmunk.

"Pleased to meet you," she replied, briefly glancing up but without slowing down her knife work as she carved lemon wedges into intricate geometric patterns. She wore the red necktie of a supervisor.

"Mr. Lassard is a passenger at one of my tables in the Pelican Room. He's also a detective with the police," Niels said. "He'd like to speak with Ricki about the *incident*. He wants to help."

A large-boned young woman wearing a blue necktie looked at Damon.

Roberta set down her knife and turned to the woman. "Ricki, why don't you go on break. Take the detective to the bussing station on deck number four. There shouldn't be anyone down there at this time of day."

Damon followed Ricki out of the room and into a wide hallway. Thirty feet down the hall, the floor transitioned from linoleum to slippery metal and the temperature dropped at least thirty degrees. "These are the meat lockers," Ricki said over her shoulder. They passed windowless metal doors bearing the designations "beef," "poultry," and "fish." Painted red boxes resembling hockey creases marked the floor spaces in front of the lockers. "So no one gets crushed by someone opening the door from the inside," Ricki explained even though Damon hadn't asked. A black man in a blue mechanic's uniform and a black ski cap rolled a cart loaded with boxes labeled "lamb loin" and "turkey bacon" past them in the opposite direction. As Damon followed Ricki around a bend in the hallway, they passed an open door providing a view into the butchers' quarters. Two men in stained aprons and winter hats wielded knives over industrial-sized acrylic cutting boards. A third manned a meat grinder. The butchers' breath was visible. Damon held his nose to ward off the odor.

They reached an interior stairwell. Damon stepped down with caution—it was narrower and twice as steep as the staircases on board for passengers.

The bussing station on the fourth deck—where wait staff cleared leftover food from plates and refilled water pitchers and soft drinks—was a ghost town.

"I need to start by telling you I'm not a police detective, yet," Damon said. He perched on an uncomfortable metal stool. Ricki leaned against a sink shaped like a trough, only wider.

"So what are you doing here?" she asked.

"I'm a passenger who sits at the same dinner table as Jack Jackman. He's the man who bit into glass on the first night of this week's cruise. Personally, I think he planted the glass himself and is looking for a payday.

I've solved some pretty big crimes in the past, and I start training at my local police academy in the United States in a few weeks. I'm not here to get anyone in trouble, unless it's Jack. If you broke a glass that night, no problem with me. I'll never say a word. But I need to know for sure, because if you didn't break one and don't know of someone who did, I'm going to keep looking for evidence to contradict Jack's claim."

Ricki's itty-bitty eyelashes flickered. "That's really good of you, Mr. Lassard. I don't want to get fired, especially for something I didn't do. I'll tell you the same thing I told the Pelican Room's headwaiter, the executive chef, and cruise line's attorney: I didn't break a single glass on Sunday night, and I don't know anyone in the area who did."

"Were you the only person handling potatoes?"

"I didn't do the peeling, chopping, or boiling. But after the potatoes were cooked, I was the only one who touched them through plating." She pulled the hair net off of her head. Thin, bottled blond hair fell to her shoulders. "The potatoes are boiled in cubes, about an inch on each side, and they come to me in huge tubs. I add hot butter, cream, and milk, then salt, pepper, and a touch of paprika. After that, I run the mixture through my potato whipper."

Damon cocked his head to one side—an unspoken question mark.

"It's a contraption with a wide-mouthed, stainless-steel bowl, only the bottom has holes like a colander. When I turn the machine's crank, it rotates a pair of paddle-shaped blades that whip the potatoes smooth and press them down through the holes. You mount the whole thing on top of a larger bowl that collects the whipped potatoes."

"How big are the holes?" Damon asked.

"Pretty small. Maybe the size of a dimple on a golf ball. Not a whole lot different than a strainer you'd use for draining pasta, but the holes are closer together. More like a honeycomb."

"Are the holes large enough for a shard of glass to fit through?"

"No way," Ricki said without hesitation. "I would have felt grinding when I was turning the crank."

"So if Jack Jackman had been served potatoes with glass in them, the shards would have to be hidden inside after they were mashed."

"Whipped," Ricki corrected, "but yes. And after whipping, I was the only one who scooped the potatoes onto the entrée plates."

"Were the potatoes the last thing on the plates before they were served on Sunday night?"

"Second to last. For all three potato dishes."

Damon stared at Ricki blankly.

"There are six specials each night in addition to the five standard entrées we serve every evening," she explained. "On the Sunday menu, three of the eleven dishes came with potatoes."

Damon nodded with understanding. "So after you put potatoes on the plates, where did they go?"

"To the station right next to me. Steamed asparagus. All three potato entrées on Sunday—salmon, beef Wellington, and chicken Marsala—came with asparagus. The executive chef designs the dishes so we can get plates out the door quickly."

"That makes sense," Damon said. "And you didn't see or hear the person on asparagus break any glass?"

"I didn't. There wasn't any glass at either of our stations."

"And once plating was finished, where did the entrées go?" Damon rested his chin on one fist.

"Adriana, she was on asparagus, covered the plates with lids and stacked them on the carts. A different cart for each entrée. Once a cart's full, a kitchen staffer takes it to a holding area where the waiters pull off the dishes they need for their tables."

"So there was a period of time when the plates were out of your sight before the passengers were served."

"Of course," Ricki said. "But they should've been covered by a lid the whole time and wouldn't be touched by anyone working with glass."

"This is very helpful, Ricki. Thank you."

"I really need this job, Mr. Lassard," Ricki said with a pleading look in her eyes.

"I'll do everything I can to help. And, please, call me Damon."

At his request, Ricki showed Damon the potato-whipping area. He noticed a line of four waste bins along a wall—one for food waste, paper and plastic, metal and aluminum, and bottles and glass. Damon pointed to them.

"All of the prep stations have those," Ricki explained. "On Sunday night, after I heard about what happened to Mr. Jackman, I checked the bottles-and-glass bin here at the station. It was empty."

"How often is the trash collected?" Damon asked.

"A couple of times a day. They go to the ship's waste and recycling facility. It's right next to this galley."

"So any broken glass would end up there?"

"I believe so," she said.

To be thorough, Damon asked Ricki to take him to see the garbage.

"Almost all of the trash on board is incinerated," the manager of waste services explained after they arrived. "But the glass is recycled. First, we separate everything that comes in." He pointed to six rolling carts: two with green glass, two with ceramics and brown glass, and two with clear glass. Each was large enough to hold the collective volume of seven or eight shopping carts and was three-quarters full. "We recycle each week on Saint Martin," the manager said. "That's our stop on Thursday."

In theory, Damon thought, the remainder of the broken glass that wound up on Jack Jackman's plate could be in one of the carts of clear glass in front of him. But they contained thousands of bottles and shards. Hunting through them was a dangerous task that wouldn't provide any additional information. Damon thanked the waste-services manager for his time, then Ricki showed him the way out.

"Thank you for trying to help," she said. "If there's anything else you need, just call me." She gave Damon her room's telephone number.

* * *

Damon stood in his stateroom shower, two days into his vacation, with his mind racing. Hot beads of water pelted his face. Had he concocted two mysteries that didn't exist? No. Damon was certain that Jack, assisted by Fava, had planted glass in his own food. That was more of a conundrum than a mystery—how to prove the occurrence of an event when there was no evidence to be found.

Philippa's death, on the other hand, *was* a mystery. Everyone but Damon—and the killer, of course—believed it had been a suicide. He suspected that even his mother, who was intrigued by the Drummiller family history, didn't believe one of their tablemates had done away with Philippa.

But the motives were piling up, Damon thought. After his and Lynne's breakfast conversation with Houston, Raymond Carmichael had crept up Damon's suspect list. Miles had swooped in and scooped up the major client Raymond had been courting—effectively cementing Raymond's departure from Drummiller Box and Board and driving a stake into any hope he had for a share of the business. But that only pitted Raymond against Miles. And if Miles was sleeping with Vicky, as Damon suspected, that would deepen Raymond's motive to kill Miles, not Philippa. Unless, of course, Raymond wanted to punish the whole Drummiller family and Philippa was his selected delegate. Or perhaps he intended to pick off the family members one by one, and Philippa was simply the first.

Chapter 10

Damon and Lynne reached their seats in the Pelican Room before any of their tablemates. The Tuesday evening menu looked particularly appetizing. Insalata caprese, shrimp cocktail, and lobster tail tangled with French onion soup, escargot, and a veal chop for Damon's attention.

The Carmichaels and elder Drummillers arrived in turn, followed by Jack and Fava, and finally by Amanda. Fava shot Damon a conspiratorial smile as she sat. Damon forced a disingenuous one in return.

"Where's Candice?" Houston asked Amanda after everyone at the table had ordered.

"How should I know?"

"You two are sharing a stateroom."

"True. But I didn't come from there. I dressed over an hour ago and caught the comedy act before dinner."

"Miles, have you seen Candice?" Houston asked.

"Not since lunchtime," he replied. "Maybe she went to the buffet dinner at the Galleon."

"My guess is she's at the Irish pub with the bartender she was talking about," Amanda said.

"You're probably right," Houston grumbled. "Amanda, would you go fetch her? I'd like us to eat together as a family. It's the only time all day we're all together on this ship."

Amanda pouted silently but followed her father's request and left the table in search of her niece.

She returned less than ten minutes later. As she approached her seat, she ran a finger along the back of

Damon's collar. His neck tingled at the unexpected touch.

"The bartender said he hasn't seen her all day," Amanda said to the group.

"Are you sure you spoke to the right one, dear?" Kitty asked.

"I'm sure. I described Candice to one of the waitresses. She pointed out the bartender Candice had been flirting with. But according to the waitress, Candice started talking to another guy last night. He was dressed as a passenger but put their drinks on a crew card."

"What's that?" Lynne asked Amanda.

"It's like the SeaPass cards we have, but for crew. The waitress said it's a different color."

"Did the waitress know this man?" Kitty asked.

"She said she hadn't seen him before," Amanda said. "And according to her, the bartender was pretty jealous."

"Just like men—they can't accept when they've lost control of a woman," Vicky said.

Raymond stared at the table, as if he'd like to crawl through the floor.

"That reminds me of the noun and verb that were dating," Lynne said. "But the verb broke it off. The noun was too possessive."

* * *

After dinner, the Drummillers and Carmichaels agreed to walk the ship in search of Candice. Damon suspected the family wanted to verify that Candice hadn't done something rash in response to her mother's death. They split into two sets of three and set off. Damon and Lynne weren't invited to join the search, nor were Jack and Fava. The couple from Dallas said they were going to take in a high-diving show at the aquatics theater. Damon thought he and Lynne could tackle karaoke night at the Crooner, but his mother had other plans. She'd met a divorced dentist from Albuquerque that afternoon, and was meeting him at Foxtrot—a ballroom dance club that catered to the fifty-and-older set.

Damon passed an hour in the casino. He was at a blackjack table, down thirty dollars, when he saw Houston walking in his direction with Amanda and Raymond in tow.

"Still no sign of her?" Damon asked as they neared.

Houston stopped and shook his head. "No. Guest Services made an announcement over the public-address system, but she still hasn't surfaced. Security has her name and photo now, but we're at sea, so there's not much they'll do. 'She has to show up somewhere,' is all they said."

Unless she went overboard, too.

Houston walked off, angrily mumbling to himself. Amanda let Raymond pass by her, winked at Damon, and mouthed, "Stop by my room later tonight." And then the search party was gone.

If Amanda has in mind what I think she does, I hope they don't find Candice first. Damon chastised himself as soon as the thought crossed his mind—Candice could be hurt, even dead. He should help find her.

He headed to a house phone near the casino bar and called Ricki, the potato whipper. To his surprise, she picked up.

"Ricki? This is Damon Lassard. We met earlier today."

"Did you find out something?"

"About the glass? No, not yet. Listen, I have a favor I need to ask you. One of my tablemates has gone missing. She's been hanging out in the Irish pub and has gotten to know some of the people who are working there. I was wondering if there are any spots in the crew-only area where she might be."

"There are three bars down here. Give me fifteen minutes to freshen up, and I'll take you around. But keep up the façade you used with Niels—you're with the police if anyone asks. I could get in trouble for bringing a passenger into crew quarters."

* * *

With a swipe of her black SeaPass card, Ricki led Damon into the crew-only area. Damon explained the pub waitress's story about the man she'd seen Candice with the previous evening.

"That seems strange," Ricki said. "Other than the officers, crew aren't allowed in the passenger bars."

She first led Damon to the mess hall on the third deck—cruise ship food in a hospital-cafeteria setting. A smattering of people ate in small clusters, some in uniform, others in casual clothes. Candice wasn't among them.

"Is this Candice girl a smoker?" Ricki asked.

"Not that I know of."

"Okay, then let's hit the two nonsmoking crew bars first. There's a club on this deck called Disco and a quiet English pub upstairs. If we strike out, we can try DeGas—that's an open-air bar where the smokers congregate. We have big parties there but nothing's scheduled for tonight. There's a coffee shop and a game room we can try, too."

First they hit Disco, where blue vinyl-backed chairs surrounded low tables. The seats were empty save for a pair of young Asian girls in sequined tops who were laughing loudly. To one side, strobe lights beat down on a parquet floor devoid of dancers. A small bar, however, was cramped with a brassy crowd, but there was no sign of Candice.

"Do you know all of the crew?" Damon asked Ricki as they approached the bar. He had to shout to be heard over the music pumping out of overhead speakers.

"Not even close," she shouted back. "There are about two thousand of us. I know the crew who work in the formal dining galley, a lot of the waiters, and some of the other food-prep staff from the other galleys. It's like a small college campus: you know the people who are in your classes, everyone else is just a face." Ricki pressed toward the bar through a seam that opened between two patrons.

"But the guys tending the crew bars know everyone," she said to Damon over her shoulder and laughed.

"Poppy! How's life tonight?" Ricki asked a bartender who gave her a wide-mouthed smile. With his baby-smooth, mocha skin, Poppy didn't look a day over eighteen. A jauntily placed sailor's cap made Damon think Popeye rather than Poppy.

"Life's good, Miss Ricki. Who's the tall stalk of celery?" To Damon he said, "I haven't seen you around. Are you new?"

"Actually, I'm a passenger," Damon said.

"He's with the police," Ricki added quickly. Her voice was barely audible over the music and boisterous throng of crew.

"The police?" Poppy responded. "Sounds positively exciting, Miss Ricki. Does this have anything to do with that little glass incident?"

"You know I can't talk about that, Poppy." She winked at him. "But I'd appreciate it if you could let him ask you a few questions, seeing as you know everything that goes on down here."

"It would be my pleasure. Just let me pour beers for the laundry guys at the end of the bar first."

Poppy returned three minutes later and slid tumblers filled with a yellowish-brown liquid in front of Damon and Ricki. "Whiskey sours, on the house," he stated. "Passenger SeaPass cards don't work down here, and I wouldn't think of charging Miss Ricki when she's helping the police."

Damon reached into his wallet and pulled out a twenty. He slid it across the bar. "If I'm breaking protocol by being down here, I might as well break the no-cash-on-board rule, too."

Poppy grinned. "Never met a Jackson I didn't like. Janet or Andrew."

"I'm looking for a passenger," Damon said, moving the conversation to the business at hand. "A girl who just turned twenty-one. Her name's Candice Drummiller and one of the waitresses at the Irish pub on the promenade saw her with a man who was dressed in casual clothes but had a crew SeaPass card."

"So either someone was breaking protocol by cavorting with a guest in the passenger area," Ricki said, "or it was an officer. But according to Mr. Lassard here, the waitress didn't recognize the guy. And we all know who the officers are, at least by sight." She sipped her whiskey sour through a straw.

"Rich college girl with a sullen attitude and lots of jewelry?" Poppy asked.

"That sounds like her," Damon said.

"Then I've solved the mystery." Poppy snapped his fingers. "The guy she was with wasn't an officer. He's one of the doctors."

Ricki smacked her head.

"I don't get it," Damon said.

"We have a sick bay for passengers and crew," Ricki explained. "More like a mini–emergency room. There are two doctors and three nurses on board at any given time. The docs have officers' privileges, like the right to hang out in the passenger areas when they're off duty. That's why the guy Candice was with in the pub wasn't wearing a uniform but had a crew SeaPass card."

"And the doctors rotate on and off of the ship every four to six months," Poppy added. "Which would explain why the waitress didn't recognize him."

Ricki nodded. "If he's only been on board for a month or two, and she hasn't been sick, they may not have crossed paths."

"But you know him, right Poppy?" Damon asked.

"Man, I know everybody who works on this ship. There's not a staffer on board who doesn't come in here for a drink. Even the few who don't *partake* come here to hang out."

"So you saw Candice and the doctor here tonight?"

Damon waited patiently as Poppy silently wiped down a pair of empty pint glasses. Damon took the hint and laid another twenty-dollar bill on the bar.

"They left fifteen minutes before you walked in," Poppy said. "He's Johnny Walker."

"That's his name or what he drinks?" Damon asked.

"What he drinks, man. Johnny Walker. But we only carry the red and black labels. No Johnny Walker blue."

"Any idea what the doctor's name is?"

"I said I know everybody, didn't I?"

Damon tapped his fingers on the bar.

"Doc Amboy," Poppy said after a moment. "Joseph Amboy. Young guy from Georgia. Big lug. You wouldn't think he was a doctor by the looks of him—more like a linebacker."

"Any idea where they went from here?" Ricki asked and finished her whiskey sour.

"The doc didn't tell me, but I have a guess. There's only one reason a crew member risks his job by bringing a passenger down here. To get L-A-I-D."

Damon gave the young bartender a hard stare.

"Unless you're escorting the police, of course," Poppy said with a smile.

"Did you overhear any of their conversation?" Damon asked.

"A little. They were talking about the ice box."

Damon raised his eyebrows.

Poppy looked to either side, then whispered. "That's the freezer down in the medical center where the docs can store a dead body."

* * *

"The sick bay will be closed this late at night," Ricki said before she and Damon parted ways. She had walked him out of the crew area. "I'm not sure what you're planning to do, but I'm going to leave you now—I've broken enough rules for one night."

Damon thanked Ricki profusely. Feeling indebted to her, he promised himself he'd find evidence of Jack's ploy.

The medical center occupied a large space on the ship's second deck. According to a sign on the door, regular office hours ended at eight o'clock. It was already half past ten.

Damon put his ear to the door and listened. He thought he heard a murmur but couldn't be certain. He placed a hand on the door handle and twisted. To his surprise, it opened.

Damon slipped inside and soundlessly closed the door behind him. The waiting room was dark but for a horizontal glimmer of light beneath an interior door. As he tiptoed toward the light, he heard a pair of voices. One he recognized as Candice's.

"Thank you so much, Joseph," Candice said. "Can you give me a couple of minutes alone? I'd like to say good-bye to my mother in private."

Before he could hear Joseph Amboy's reply, Damon scampered behind a patient intake desk and tucked himself underneath. The desk had a closed front blocking his view. But it backed up to a wall so as long as Dr. Amboy didn't try to sit behind it, Damon would be safe from detection.

Moments later, he heard movement. Someone, presumably Amboy, had entered the waiting room through the interior door and sat down. The room remained dark. Damon heard a faint scratching sound, and he envisioned the doctor scraping at his teeth with a nail.

A few minutes later, Candice called, "I'm done. Thank you, Joseph."

Damon heard ruffling. "Not here," Candice protested. "My dead mother is less than thirty feet away."

"Okay, okay," Joseph said. "Let's go to my stateroom. I have a bottle of wine left over from Christmas."

Feet shuffled and Damon heard the pair of would-be lovers flit out of the medical facility, shutting the door behind them. He waited in his crouch for five full minutes to ensure that neither Candice nor the young physician returned. Then, leaving the lights off, Damon gingerly stepped toward the interior door, holding his hands out like Frankenstein. "The best device for finding furniture in the dark is your shin," his mother always said.

The interior door was ajar. Damon stepped inside, shut the door behind him, and groped the wall for a switch. He found one and flipped it on. Light bathed a wide hallway with a worn carpet. Small examination rooms flanked his left and right. Near the end of the hall stood three closed doors, one facing Damon and one at either side. He stepped forward. The door to the left, labeled "office," was locked. The door at the end opened to a small surgical suite. Damon scanned it quickly but didn't see evidence of an "ice box." The door to the right had a placard that read "storage." It was unlocked.

Chapter 11

Damon turned on a light switch in the storage room. Sundry medical supplies lined the walls on cheap storage racks. A metal door beckoned him from the back of the room. It looked to be the same make as the meat lockers Damon had seen in the galley. He approached it, took a deep breath, and twisted the handle.

An overhead fluorescent light automatically crackled to life as Damon pushed open the door. A wave of air smacked him in the face. Cave cold. Damon entered the room, leaving a foot wedged between the door and its jamb. The room was just large enough for a single metal gurney—its occupant shrouded from head to foot with a gray car cover that touched down to the floor.

Damon knew the door to the ice box was unlocked, but his nerves bettered him. He backed out, found a wheelchair in the storage area, and maneuvered it into position to serve as a doorstop. Then Damon shimmied timidly along the wall to the head of the sheet-covered body resting on the gurney. He had a flash of fear as he imagined uncovering the face before him and looking down at someone other than Philippa. Damon shook his head—this was no horror movie.

He delicately pulled down the sheet and screamed.

Philippa lay under the sheet, but wide-open brown eyes stared up at him. A zombie. Damon clapped a hand over his mouth. He took a deep breath, his nostrils filling with an unpleasant mix of formaldehyde and alcohol. Surely, the doctor had closed Philippa's eyes.

Candice had probably opened them as a twisted joke—a parting gift to Joseph Amboy.

Damon reached out a quivering hand and lowered Philippa's eyelids, then pulled the sheet down to Philippa's feet. He examined her naked, lifeless body. Her skin glistened with a waxy sheen. A small set of black sutures crisscrossed the inside of Philippa's left thigh, presumably from the embalming procedure. Damon couldn't identify any other marks on the front of her body. He used the sheet to turn Philippa onto her stomach—no easy task in a tight space with a body north of 120 pounds. Black moles spotted Philippa's back like a tortilla. But Damon didn't see any knife wounds or gashes. What had he expected to find—a ragged tear from a Bowie knife that the police and the ship's physician had both overlooked?

Damon wrenched the body back to its original position. *It didn't look like she was killed before going overboard,* he thought. But someone could've given her a good shove when Philippa was leaning, unsuspecting, against the ship's railing.

Damon's thoughts shifted to Candice. What was she doing in here? Had she simply wanted to say good-bye to her mother in person before the funeral? Or had she done something else? The body was bare so Candice hadn't planted anything on it. Had something been removed?

Damon checked under Philippa's fingernails. They looked clean. *That could be due to the hours she spent in the water,* he thought, but more likely there hadn't been a struggle.

As he covered Philippa's body, he noticed a cardboard box in the corner behind the propped-open door. Damon bent down and pulled open rigid flaps— inside were personal belongings. He sat down cross-legged on the floor, his back against the wheelchair, and removed the box's contents: a gray cardigan and white blouse, dark jeans, a wallet, and a single flip-flop.

Damon leafed through Philippa's waterlogged wallet: a stack of credit cards but zero cash—any bills may have been pinched by one of Inspector Albury's subordinates.

Philippa's clothes smelled like a wet dog bathed in sea salt. Damon uncrumpled the jeans, stiff from air drying. Inside the right front pocket, he found a note. Damon recalled hearing the police officer's staticky voice on Albury's walkie-talkie: There had been a paper note, and the gist of the officer's message was that the words were unreadable due to water-soaked ink.

Damon carefully unfolded the paper. A short paragraph of blue smears was visible on *Vitamin of the Seas* stationary. *The Bahamian police officer hadn't inspected the note too closely*, Damon thought. Either that, or something had been lost in the garbled transmission, because toward the bottom of the inky blotch, he could distinguish blurry letters that appeared to spell out "meet me."

Meet me. Damon contemplated the ramifications of the words. To his mind, the meaning was clear: Someone had asked Philippa to meet him or her in the middle of the night in a secluded spot at the very back of the ship. And Philippa had gone.

Damon deleted Candice from his list of suspects. If she'd killed her mother, she'd have taken the note.

He ticked off the remaining potential murderers on his fingers: Houston, Kitty, Miles, Amanda, Raymond, and Vicky.

Damon tucked the note back into the pocket of Philippa's jeans, replaced her belongings in the box, and split from the medical center.

* * *

Damon showered the smell of salt water and embalming fluids from his body, spritzed on cologne, and dressed in khaki pants and an open-necked navy polo. As he approached Amanda's stateroom, he noticed that Philippa's room next door wasn't barred by police tape.

Amanda answered Damon's knock wearing nothing but a sheer-pink baby-doll nightgown and a black-satin choker highlighted by a marquise-cut pink topaz. Her lustrous dark hair cascaded down along a delicate jawline and fell behind her snow-white shoulders. Damon caught his breath.

"Candice isn't here?" Damon asked to break the ice, though he knew the answer.

"No, but she's safe," Amanda said and playfully tugged Damon into the room by his collar. "She called fifteen minutes ago and said she wouldn't be sleeping here tonight. Good for her." Amanda smiled and closed the door behind Damon. "And good for us."

She laid a hand flat against his chest. "I had room service bring a bottle of wine." Amanda moved to the small sofa, sat to one side, and patted the space beside her. "Be a dear and pour us a couple of glasses. I want to feel warm and tingly in more ways than one."

Damon uncorked the bottle, then sat next to Amanda and poured two heavy measures. He knew it was a bad idea to get involved with someone he considered a murder suspect. But his break up with Bethany, the weather girl back home, hit him hard and he craved physical attention.

As they clinked glasses, Damon's eyes settled on the door adjoining Amanda and Candice's stateroom with the one next door—Philippa's. Other than the front door, it was the only access point to Philippa's room. Damon had seen Inspector Albury verify that Philippa's interior door was locked, but the inspector's presence had stymied Damon from scrutinizing it closely. His mind bounced back-and-forth between Amanda's hand on his thigh and the interior door. Damon steadied his resolve. Solving this murder was more important to him than satiating his desires. Then again, maybe he could have his cake and eat it, too.

Sixty seconds into heavy kissing and light touching, Damon fabricated an accident. Still holding his glass in one hand, he reached both arms around Amanda's upper back, as if to release the tie on her nightgown, and purposefully spilled red wine down her back.

"Ahh," Amanda shouted.

"I'm so sorry." Damon hastily unwound their bodies. "I'm such a klutz. Let me grab some Kleenex." Damon stepped quickly into the tiny bathroom and yanked a handful of tissues from the box. He returned and dabbed at Amanda's back, then grimaced at the sight of a magenta stain on the sofa.

"No worries," Amanda said, catching his eye with a smile. She flipped over the couch cushion. "Good as new. But my back's all sticky. It'll be a tight fit, but maybe you can soap me down in the shower?"

"I think I can manage that," Damon said. "I got a little wine in your hair, too. Why don't you rinse that out, and I'll join you in a couple of minutes."

"Sounds good," Amanda moved toward the bathroom door. She paused before entering, pulled the tie behind her back, and let her nightgown fall to the floor. Amanda looked back over her shoulder at Damon. "Give me three minutes, then come on in." She stepped into the bathroom and closed the door behind her.

Damon was temporarily frozen by the curve of Amanda's figure. But as soon as the shower water began to run, he sprang into action.

Damon examined the interior door connecting Amanda's room with Philippa's. A button on the handle was pushed-in and positioned horizontally. He quietly rattled the handle to confirm it was locked. As he twisted the button to the vertical position, it popped out and he heard a click, like a bolt shooting back from the jamb, unlocking the door. Damon pulled it open. Facing him was the flat backside of a second door—one to Philippa's room. Damon pushed. It was still locked.

To pass between adjoining rooms, Damon concluded, each of the interior doors had to be unlocked from its own side. He recalled Amanda and Candice telling Inspector Albury that neither of them had opened their interior door. Was that true? Did it even matter—neither could've accessed Philippa's room without her adjoining door being unlocked as well.

Damon considered the "suicide" note Inspector Albury had found in Philippa's nightstand drawer. In his opinion, there were only three ways a killer could have left it there: Philippa allowed the murderer into her room, the killer used one of the six key cards that opened the stateroom's front door, or the person who left the "suicide" note somehow passed into Philippa's cabin through the set of two interior doors connecting her room with the one Damon was standing in.

"Okay, Damon," Amanda called from the shower. "I'm ready for you."

Damon knew he'd regret it later, but he didn't have the willpower to resist. He pushed all thoughts of constraint to the recesses of his mind and joined Amanda.

* * *

Ninety minutes later, Damon returned to the stateroom he shared with his mother. He showered away the musty smell of sex before quietly settling into the pull-out sofa under a blanket. Lynne was asleep in the bed under a tightly tucked sheet, her breath inaudible.

Damon remonstrated himself for giving in to his temptations. But he was a single man. Why should he pass up a night of pleasure? Because she could be a murderess—albeit a particularly salacious one, he reminded himself with a grin.

He tried to sleep, but every time he shut his eyes, Philippa's open, dead eyes stared up at him. Her eyes wouldn't let him go—turning from dead, to feral, and back to dead again.

The words "meet me" flashed through his thoughts, followed by a vision of Philippa's waxy fingers and clean fingernails. Her fingertips.

Fingertips!

Damon bolted upright in bed, the pistons in his brain firing. But his thoughts were no longer focused on Philippa. Rather, they centered on Fava—her slender fingers and perfectly shaped, french-tipped fingernails. When he and Fava had entered the Lion's Crown for a drink the previous evening, she'd winced as she rubbed Purell between her fingers. But the sanitizer wasn't cold. No, Damon reasoned, Fava reacted because her finger burned. A small cut from breaking a champagne flute might not be visible to the naked eye, but it couldn't hide from the antiseptic properties of Purell.

* * *

Wednesday, January 15

Damon woke at eight o'clock. Sunlight beaming through the parted curtains warmed his back. He popped his head up and looked over at the bed.

"Good morning, sunshine," his mother said. She was sitting upright, legs hidden under the sheet. Her face was obscured by a paperback.

Damon yawned. "What are you reading?"

"It's a book on antigravity. Simply impossible to put down."

"Ha-ha." Damon sat up and rubbed his eyes.

"You were out late last night." Lynne set the book in her lap. "Not that it's any of my business. You can do whatever you want." She paused, then added, "Did you do whatever you wanted?"

Damon ignored his mother's tongue-in-cheek comment and, instead, brought her up to speed on his discovery of Candice and the note in Philippa's pocket.

"Meet me," Lynne said when he finished. "Sounds pretty straightforward. I thought the police said the note was indecipherable."

"It was blurry," Damon admitted. "The word *meet* could have been *week* or maybe *meek*. But the *me* part seemed pretty clear, so *meet* makes the most sense."

"Are you sure those were the full words?" Lynne asked. "Could *me* have been the first two letters of a longer word?"

"I hadn't thought of that. Yes, that's certainly possible."

"And you're sure the Bahamian police saw the note?"

"I was in Philippa's stateroom with Inspector Albury when a police officer radioed him on his walkie-talkie," Damon said. "I remember the officer saying water had smeared the ink. Though, the transmission was broken up by a lot of static so I didn't catch every word."

"Did the inspector ever actually see the note?"

"Not that I'm aware of," Damon said.

Lynne rose. "I'm going to jump in the shower, then let's get some breakfast."

"Hold on. What if Candice killed her mother and planted the note last night when she was alone with Philippa?"

"You mean the note you found was different than the one the police looked at?"

"I'm not sure. I was just throwing it out there."

Lynne stopped at the door to the bathroom and shook her head. "Why would she do that? If Candice killed Philippa, why plant a suspicious note when no one is looking for a murderer?"

Lynne glided into the bathroom and shut the door behind her. *Candice may not have stuffed the note into Philippa's pocket*, Damon thought, *but perhaps she'd seen it.* If she had and was able to make out the words "meet me," might she have concluded that her mother was killed? And if so, Damon wondered, could he use Candice as a confidant?

* * *

Slick pavement and damp air suggested recent rain that had unfinished business. The *Vitamin* was docked in Saint Thomas, in the U.S. Virgin Islands. As they ventured into the port town of Charlotte Amalie, Damon relayed his notion to Lynne that Fava could have a small cut on one of her fingers. Before they could discuss it at length, however, they reached the town and joined a crush of tourists on the narrow sidewalks. The Diamond District of the Caribbean would have been a fitting moniker for the city center. Street-side placards boasted huge savings at countless jewelry outlets. Diamonds and tanzanite adornments dominated the display cases.

"Anything strike your fancy, mother?" Damon asked as they peered into a fingerprint-clouded glass case in Diamonds International. Shoppers from six cruise ships swarmed about them like ants. Damon felt like a twenty-two-year-old who had pushed his way to the bar at a fashionable Manhattan nightclub.

"Are you kidding?" Lynne said. "Everything here strikes my fancy."

"Well, pick something out, then. I'll get it for you."

Lynne turned to face her son. "I don't think so. Parents should support their children, not the other way around."

"This isn't support. It's a trinket."

"These are no trinkets, Damon. And I don't need any new jewelry. Both your father and Jack bought me plenty."

Jack Brown had been Lynne's second husband. He, like Damon's father, had passed away.

"How about we pick something out for Rebecca?" Lynne asked. She'd been urging Damon to date his best friend since the day he met Rebecca. In fact, Lynne had introduced them.

"I thought I'd get her a rum cake," Damon replied.

Lynne's brow puckered. "Rum cake? Give me a break. How about a simple set of earrings? They have some nice aquamarine ones in here. You can afford it."

"It's not a question of money. It's the message behind the gift."

"And, pray tell, what's the message behind a rum cake?"

"It's neutral. It doesn't mean anything."

"That's for sure. Think it over, Damon. We're in Saint Martin tomorrow, and then that's it. Just two days at sea after that before we return to Miami."

Chapter 12

Damon spotted Candice on the sixteenth deck, which overlooked the ship's pools on the deck below. She lay flat on her back, eyes closed, the sun's rays baking her scantily clad body. She lacked the womanly curves that genetics had bestowed on her aunt Amanda. Instead, Candice looked bloated. Her puffy cheeks had broken out with acne, and her sunburned arms reminded Damon of skinny sausage ropes.

The sunbathing deck was busy but not packed. Damon sat on the end of a lounge chair next to Candice, setting a beach bag beside him.

"I'm getting a drink. Would you like one?"

Candice opened a single eye. "Sure. Drink of the day is called a Lava Flow."

Damon caught the attention of one of the ubiquitous waiters circling the deck and ordered a pair of Lava Flows.

"Excellent choice, sir," the man said in a Jamaican accent, taking Damon's SeaPass card. "Best coconut rum in the Caribbean is right here on the ship."

Damon propped his chair into a position that was halfway between upright and fully reclined. The inside of his polo shirt scratched the stubble on his cheeks as he pulled it off over his head. He'd forgotten to shave in the morning.

"Would you rub some sunscreen on my back?" Damon asked.

Candice sat up. "You work fast, huh? Amanda last night and now me."

Damon could feel his cheeks flush. "I just don't want my back to burn," he stammered.

"I'm just giving you a hard time. You're what—in your thirties? Too old for me."

Damon winced. "So your aunt told you?" he asked.

"She did." Candice took a bottle of SPF 15 from Damon's outstretched hand. "No judgment here. I had company of my own last night."

Damon decided to play dumb as he turned away from Candice. "The bartender from the Irish Pub?" he asked, looking over his shoulder.

Candice squirted a palmful of sunscreen into her hand and slapped it on Damon's back. He squirmed from the cold. "Sissy," she teased as she rubbed.

"I was with the ER doctor," Candice said. "He just finished his residency and is spending a few months on the ship before settling into practice. I wanted to see my mother's body, and the only way I could figure out how to do that was by letting the doc see my body."

Damon stayed silent.

"Sorry, that sounded vulgar," Candice said.

"You couldn't wait until we got back to Miami?" Damon asked.

"No. As much as I hated her sometimes, she is, I mean was, my mother. I needed some closure."

The waiter returned and handed Damon a pair of red-and-white striped drinks in tall hurricane glasses. Candice took her hands off of Damon's back and wiped excess sunscreen on her towel. "Thanks, Candice," Damon said and set the drinks on the cement between his chair and hers, then signed a payment slip.

"Thank you." Candice picked up a Lava Flow.

Once the waiter departed, Damon decided to take a swing for the fences. "Do you mind if I ask you a question?"

Candice shrugged her shoulders.

"When the police inspector was searching your mother's stateroom," Damon said, "I heard him get a transmission on his walkie-talkie. The officer on the other end said he found a note in your mother's pocket. Did you happen to see it last night?"

"No," Candice replied. She plucked sunglasses from a tote bag and put them on. "Where would I have seen that?"

Damon breathed in deeply. "I figured your mother's personal effects might have been with her."

"Not that I saw. If there was a note, I'm sure the police took it. Why do you ask?"

Damon reached for his Lava Flow and took a long sip. It was too sweet for his taste. "I'm just curious. To be honest, ever since I saw your mother's suicide note, I've been a bit intrigued by your family."

Candice stifled a laugh. My family, intriguing. That's rich. My mother's note didn't say anything any of us didn't already know."

Damon waited. He felt like a psychologist using silence as a tactic to solicit additional information.

"Her note named me, my father, and my grandfather," Candice said. "She hasn't liked my grandfather for as long as I can remember. I'm not exactly sure why—probably because she wanted his money. Mother always wanted more to spend while she was 'still young.' As for my father, she loathed him. Probably because he's been sleeping with Vicky. I can't believe my father had the gall to invite her on this trip. A doxy, that's what my grandmother calls her."

"A doxy?" Damon repeated.

"Tramp, trollop, slut, you name it. But Grandmother wouldn't use words as unrefined as those."

Damon grinned. He'd been right about Miles and Vicky. "Your whole family knows that your father is having an affair with Vicky?" Damon asked.

"Probably. So does Raymond. It's been going on for about six months—they don't do a very good job of hiding it."

"Why didn't your mother leave him?"

Candice laughed. "That would never happen. As much as she moaned about wanting more money, she knew where her bread was buttered. She may have made my father's home life hell, but she'd never leave him."

"And your father knew it?"

"Of course. Vicky's not his first mistress."

"Did Raymond stand up to Vicky when he found out?" Damon asked.

"You ask a lot of questions."

"Sorry, I was just curious."

"Did Raymond tell off Vicky? I don't know. He's pretty weak-willed, so I doubt it." She sipped her Lava Flow, set it back down, and laid on her stomach. "How about you return the favor?"

Damon looked at Candice in confusion.

She looked up at him. "My back, dummy."

* * *

Damon was already dressed for dinner when his mother bounded into their stateroom. A print floral dress bobbed about her knees.

"Why so chipper?" Damon asked.

"Maybe because I'm on a glorious ship in the middle of the Caribbean with my son," she replied with a devilish grin. "Or maybe you should take a look at the photos I just snapped." Lynne tossed a smart phone toward Damon with an underhand throw.

Damon scanned Lynne's most recent set of pictures. Close-up snapshots of a woman's hand showed a small, vertical cut on the underside of a middle finger. A slim, almost imperceptible, scab had formed. One particularly well-angled photo captured the scabbed finger and a distinctive emerald bracelet hanging loosely around the woman's wrist. The next series of shots—taken at a slight distance—depicted a bikini-clad Fava sunbathing on her stomach: her arms were stretched down along her sides, palms facing skyward. Fava's right wrist was encased by the emerald bracelet.

"How did you get these?" Damon asked.

Lynne was beaming. "I got lucky. I saw Jack and Fava lying near one of the pools. So I ran back to the room to get my phone. When I returned, they were both asleep."

"You crept up and snapped pictures?"

"I didn't even have to get too close—the zoom function is wonderful."

"So what now?" Damon wondered out loud.

"Pin Jack and Fava in a corner and show them the photos?"

Damon thought for a moment. "No." He sat down on the edge of Lynne's bed. "Fava could just make up a story—say she cut her finger on something else. Then we'll be trapped in an uncomfortable stalemate. I don't want to suffer through dinner for the rest of the week."

"Well, we have to do something. The photos are as much proof as we're likely to get."

"I'll take them to Captain Harris. He can send them to the cruise line's attorneys. Maybe they can use them for their defense."

"Or convince Jack not to sue at all."

Damon smiled. "We didn't get a confession from Jack or Fava, but I think we've done as much as we possibly can. I only wish we could do more to solve Philippa's murder."

"You mean suicide," Lynne corrected.

"No, Mother, I mean murder, and you know it. Someone sent Philippa a letter calling for a late-night rendezvous in a remote location on the ship."

"Actually," Lynne countered, "the note just said 'meet me.' Or 'week me' or 'meek me.' For all we know it was a letter Philippa left in her jeans from the last time she wore them."

Damon rolled his eyes.

"Okay," Lynne acquiesced. "I'll admit, there's a reasonable chance someone helped her overboard."

* * *

Damon arrived late to dinner in the Pelican Room. He'd succeeded in convincing the security officer standing guard at the bridge to allow him to see the ship's captain. Harris listened to Damon's story about Fava—including the part about finding champagne flutes hidden in Jack's underwear drawer—with keen interest. He thanked Damon with a firm handshake and downloaded the digital photos from Lynne's phone onto a laptop. The captain promised to pass along the pictures and speak with his contact at the cruise line's headquarters when they arrived in Saint Martin the following morning.

Fava smiled at Damon as he sat down, apparently still under the impression that her ruse had succeeded. Damon ignored her and favored Amanda with a grin instead. Fava sighed dramatically, clearly not used to being rebuffed.

Damon wondered whether Jack would hear about the photos—either from someone representing the cruise line or from his own attorney—before they deboarded in Miami.

"So where's Raymond?" Houston asked Vicky after appetizers had been served.

"I don't know," she replied. "I haven't seen him since this morning." Vicky shot Miles a guilty glance.

"You didn't go on shore with him?" Houston asked.

Candice suppressed a laugh. She caught Damon's eye and popped an "I told you so" wink in his direction.

Amanda, who was seated to Damon's right, laid a hand on his thigh. She leaned over and whispered, "Are you flirting with my niece? She just turned twenty-one, you know."

Before Damon could manufacture a response, Vicky said to Houston, "Raymond told me he had a business meeting lined up in Saint Thomas and he'd see me at dinner."

"Business?" Houston asked in disbelief. "Raymond fixes machinery at a plastics factory. What kind of business could he possibly have on a little island in the Caribbean?"

"I don't know," Vicky retorted. "I'm just repeating what he told me. I wanted some time alone anyway." She focused her gaze on her roasted peach soup. Vicky's face was caked in heavy makeup. She wore a yellow and green flower-print dress with lace embroidery around the neck. Bony elbows jutted out of her cuffed sleeves like chicken wings.

Damon couldn't fathom what appeal she held for Miles. Had Miles started sleeping with Vicky just to rub it in Raymond's face?

"So you don't even know if he made it back on the ship?" Amanda asked Vicky. "We set sail an hour ago."

Vicky looked at her quizzically. "What do you mean? The ship wouldn't leave without him."

"Of course it would," Houston thundered. "If you're too much of an idiot not to get back on board on time, they aren't going to wait."

"Houston!" Kitty clicked her tongue. "Raymond's our godson. And he's not an idiot."

"How about underachiever?" Houston growled.

Kitty reprimanded her husband with a shake of the head.

"Tell us how you really feel, Grandfather," Candice said. "Raymond probably just didn't want to eat with us."

"I don't appreciate your tone, Candice," Houston said, "especially after you failed to join us last night. But you're probably right. I'm sure he's eating somewhere else tonight."

"Why did you invite Raymond anyway?" Candice asked him. She gave Vicky a knowing glance and mouthed an insincere "sorry."

"It was Miles's idea." Houston sighed.

"A fine idea at that," Kitty chimed in. "Raymond is like a son to us and a brother to Miles."

Lynne, who was sitting to Damon's left, surreptitiously pinched his side, just under the ribcage. Damon didn't know if she was advising him to keep his mouth closed or urging him to exploit an opening in the conversation. He chose the latter interpretation.

Damon turned his attention to Kitty and asked, "How did you and Houston become Raymond's godparents?" Amanda's fingers walked their way up his thigh. Damon cupped his hand over hers and held it firm. *How can I shake loose the information I need to solve a murder with this kind of distraction?* he thought.

Houston started to speak but Kitty placed a hand on his forearm.

"In the late '60s, Houston served in Vietnam with Raymond's father, Kenneth," she said. "They were thick as thieves, those two. When they returned to the States, Houston moved home to North Carolina and Kenneth went back to Delaware. Kenneth's father was training him to take over the family pharmacy in Wilmington. But we all saw each other a lot—mostly weekend trips to the beach, either at the Carmichaels' place on the Jersey shore or our little getaway near the Outer Banks. I became close with Kenneth's wife,

Judith. Houston and I trusted them like family. So it only made sense to act as godparents for each other's first born. It was a good thing, too."

"We would've helped Judith no matter what," Houston grumbled.

Kitty patted his hand. "Yes, dear. I know."

"What happened?" Lynne ventured.

"There was a fire at the pharmacy," Kitty said. "It happened after hours. Kenneth and his father, Buzz, were the only ones inside. Taking inventory or something like that."

"From what I read, the place went up in flames like a Roman candle," Houston said. "Buzz was a cheap SOB."

Lynne gave him a puzzled look.

"Kenneth's father didn't install overhead sprinklers," Kitty explained. "And he didn't have insurance coverage, either. All of Buzz's and Kenneth's money was tied up in the pharmacy. They lost everything. Even their beach house had been mortgaged to the hilt."

Lynne tilted her head and sighed. "So Judith was left alone with Raymond?"

"With Raymond and her mother-in-law, Edith," Kitty replied. "Raymond was all of three years old. Judith found work as a hairdresser, and Edith moved in and stayed home to watch him. They probably could have scraped by like so many people do, but Houston and I felt Judith deserved better. So we sent her a check every month until Raymond finished school. Nothing extravagant, but just enough to give them a little extra."

"That's incredibly generous," Lynne said.

Kitty smiled. "It made us feel good about ourselves," she admitted.

* * *

Forty-five minutes later, Damon and his tablemates were finishing coffee and digestifs. Jack and Fava had departed prior to dessert to take in a jazz concert. The headwaiter, Charles, approached. "Pardon me," he said with a slight bow. "Was dinner to your liking tonight?"

Everyone nodded their heads in unison.

"Very good." Charles turned his attention to Vicky. "Ms. Carmichael, I'm sorry to interrupt, but there's someone outside of the dining room who needs to speak with you."

"Is it my husband?" Vicky asked.

"No, madame. But I believe the matter concerns him."

"Well, who is it?" Miles interrupted.

Charles scanned the table. "I think Ms. Carmichael may prefer to speak with monsieur alone."

"I don't think so," Miles said and rose from his seat. "I'll go with you, Vicky."

Miles and Vicky walked briskly with Charles to the front of the dining room and then disappeared from sight.

After two minutes of stifling silence, Kitty and Lynne started an innocuous conversation about scrapbooking. Amanda leaned in close to Damon and whispered, "Want to join me for a drink in an hour?"

Damon agreed.

Five minutes later, Miles returned to the table.

"Father, would you please join us? There's a *situation*, and I think it'll help to have your assistance given your diamond-level status with the cruise line."

As Houston rose from the table, Kitty said, "Hold on." She looked at Miles. "Is Raymond on the ship?"

Miles hesitated, his eyes darting to Damon and Lynne.

"This sounds like a family issue," Lynne said. "Come on, Damon. Let's go so the Drummillers can talk in private."

"Thank you," Kitty said.

Damon and Lynne walked out of the dining room. As they left, Lynne furtively pointed to Vicky Carmichael who stood waiting in a corner just outside of the dining room's entryway with a uniformed security officer and a beefy man in an ill-fitting suit.

Once out of earshot, Lynne said, "I wonder what kind of trouble Raymond's gotten himself into."

"I should be able to find out," Damon replied. "I'm meeting Amanda for a drink."

* * *

The Noble Rot, an open-air wine bar in the park on the eighth deck, featured an array of vine-covered trellises. Amanda sat on a sleek metal stool, wearing a scarlet blouse with a sweetheart neckline coupled with a short, white, pleated skirt. Moonlight glinted off of her bare legs.

"You changed clothes since dinner," Damon said as he slid onto a stool beside her.

"Thanks for noticing." Amanda spun around to face the bar. Her calves brushed against his. She smiled. "Should we get some wine?"

After perusing the menu, Damon ordered a carafe of an Argentinean Malbec.

"I bet you're dying to know what happened to Raymond," Amanda said with a mischievous grin.

"A little," Damon admitted. "When we left the dining room, my mother and I saw Vicky with a security guard and a guy who looked like a Secret Service reject."

The bartender returned and poured two liberal glasses of wine. He set the carafe in front of them. Without toasting, they sipped the inky purple offering. It had a robust tannic taste.

"I'll tell you what I heard, just don't let on to anyone else in my family that you know. They're completely embarrassed and my parents would be mortified if they knew I told you."

Damon nodded his head. "No problem."

"Okay. I only know as much as Miles told us at the table. Then he and Father went with Vicky to see if they could spring Raymond."

"*Spring* him?"

"Ship security has him locked up," she said nonchalantly.

"There's a jail on board?"

"I'm not exactly sure. Miles said he was locked in a room next to the security office."

"What did he do?"

"Apparently, he was trying to smuggle a jar of spiders on board." Amanda's full lips parted with a giggle, showing off straight, lightly stained teeth.

Damon laughed alongside Amanda, but the wheels in his head were churning. "Did security stop him when he was reboarding?"

"Yes. Miles said Raymond was carrying a backpack. He put it on the conveyor belt, then walked through the metal detector. Something in the backpack caught the eye of the guard who was monitoring the x-ray images."

"Spiders?"

"According to Miles, five or six black ones, maybe a half-inch in size, crawling around in an empty pickle jar."

"A pickle jar?"

"That's what Miles said. Raymond claimed innocence, of course. He told security he had no idea the jar was in his backpack—someone on Saint Thomas must have put it in there by mistake."

Damon picked up his wine glass. "Did he leave the backpack on the ground somewhere?"

"I don't know," Amanda replied. She *clinked* her glass to his. "Here's to one crazy trip."

They sipped in silence. Amanda licked a trickle of wine from her upper lip. "Want to see if we can top last night?" she asked.

Chapter 13
Thursday, January 16

Damon and Lynne spent Thursday on a beach in Saint Martin. They chose a stretch of sand on Nettle Bay near Marigot, on the French-speaking side of the island. The opposite end of Saint Martin, to the south, was dominated by Dutch-speaking citizens.

The beach was quiet and the ocean calm. Mother and son lay in beach chairs under umbrellas as a light breeze cooled the hot but moistureless air. Damon was reading a John Sandford paperback and drinking Negra Modelo. Lynne concentrated on a Lawrence Block classic downloaded to her Kindle and stuck with bottled water.

"You had another late night," Lynne said.

"I was with Amanda," Damon admitted. He relayed the story Amanda told him about Raymond, then said, "I promise these last three nights on board are all yours."

Lynne laughed. "You don't have to worry about me. I can fend for myself. Even if it means you're with a woman other than Rebecca."

Damon groaned.

"Don't worry; I've decided not to push you into buying her a piece of jewelry. And any woman who makes you happy makes me happy."

"Thanks. Did you see the dentist again last night?" Damon asked.

"No, I decided he wasn't my type. But I met another very nice man at the Crooner."

"Good. You went by yourself?"

"Yes, I sat near the piano. There was a lovely crowd, and Rudy Kent—he's a physician from Boston—bought me a drink."

"And?"

"And nothing. We had a drink, sang along to some lively tunes, and then had a nice conversation. He's a widower and is on the cruise with his daughter's family."

"Are you planning to see him again?"

"Possibly. He said he's going to Shadow's Lounge tonight, so I know where to find him if you leave me to my own devices again." She laughed and squeezed Damon's forearm.

* * *

Just before one o'clock, Miles plunked a chair down in the sand beside Damon and Lynne.

"Fancy running into you two here," he said.

Lynne set down her Kindle, and Damon held up his hand in a wave. "It's one of the few beaches near the ship," he said. "I'm surprised there aren't more passengers from the *Vitamin* here."

"There are lots of other options in Saint Martin, I suppose," Miles replied. "We came once when I was a teenager. I remember going on a treetop zip-line excursion with my father. He didn't weigh as much then. Neither did I." Miles looked down at his navel. It reminded Damon of the hole at the top of a large anthill.

"Are you on your own today, Miles?" Lynne asked.

"Yes," he said hesitantly. "Though I had breakfast with Vicky this morning."

"Is Raymond all right?" Damon asked with mock concern.

Miles sprayed sunscreen onto his flabby calves. "Raymond's fine. He missed the ship last night, which is why the *Vitamin* staff wanted to speak with Vicky. My father and I arranged to have a speedboat bring him to Saint Martin this morning. I picked him up two hours ago."

Damon gave his mother a sideways glance. *Why was Miles lying?*

"Sounds like a costly mistake," Lynne said.

"That's for sure," Miles said. "It's about 120 miles between islands."

"Not to mention Raymond losing out on a night aboard the ship," Lynne said. "How did he manage to miss the boat?"

Miles flipped on sunglasses before answering. "I'm not sure," he said quickly, then added, "he probably forgot what time it was leaving."

Lynne smiled. "The first night we were on board, your father said that he hoped Candice would join you at your company when she graduates," she said, changing the subject. "I'm sure it would be nice to work with your daughter."

Miles gave a mild snort. "Unfortunately, I don't think I'll ever see her on a factory floor. Or in any of our offices, either. I've asked her every summer since she turned sixteen to work during school breaks, to start learning the business. But Candice has never shown the slightest interest in taking me up on the offer. Too much like my sister, I suspect."

"Houston wanted her to join the family business?" Damon asked with interest. He'd spent the last two nights with Amanda but realized he knew very little about her, including what she did for a living or the origin of the name "Sweet."

"He asked her to join the company when she finished college," Miles said. "Same as he did for me and Raymond. But Amanda had no interest in doing hard work." Miles blew out air. "Amanda's had my father tied around her little finger since the day she was born. She runs an online jewelry business, but I don't think she makes any real money—it's just something she does to pass the time. My father's always supported her."

"Does that bother you?" Lynne asked.

Miles shook his head and smirked. "Not really. In fact, *I'm* basically supporting her now."

"Is that so?"

"I'm the one expanding Drummiller Box and Board. My father's still the figurehead and works with his oldest clients, but I oversee the vast majority of operations. Next year, I'll take over as CEO. Amanda's money will largely stem from my efforts."

"How's that?" Damon asked despite already knowing the answer.

"A couple of ways," Miles said. "She and I will split my father's shares when my parents pass away."

So he doesn't lie about everything.

"But Amanda will have money coming to her starting next year, too," Miles explained. "My father's shares are in a trust. After he retires, the trust will make quarterly disbursements to me and Amanda. So the better I run the company, the more she benefits."

"It sounds like you're quite a benevolent brother," Lynne said. "A lesser person would feel that you should be entitled to the whole trust."

Damon admired his mother's prowess, using flattery to covertly mine for dirt.

"You hit the nail on the head, Lynne," Miles said. Before he could continue, a beach waiter stopped in front of the trio. Miles ordered a drink and bought refreshers for Damon and Lynne.

"Thank you," Lynne said. "Like I said, you're very generous."

Miles smiled. "It'll be easier now that Philippa's gone," he replied without a hint of grief. "She could spend money like the dickens, but heaven forbid I ever wanted to do something charitable. Unless, of course, it was cutting a check at a public fundraiser where she could reap the glory."

"Money can cause problems, even for those who have a lot of it," Lynne said.

"Isn't that the truth. It caused a major rift between my wife and sister. Philippa wanted Amanda completely cut out of the trust because I was the one who built up the business. And she had the gall to pester my father about it. Pretty ironic since Philippa hadn't done a day's work in years."

"That must've put your father in an awkward situation," Lynne observed.

"Perhaps, but he blew Philippa off. I suppose that's why she said my father could 'rot in hell' in her suicide note." He paused. "Over the last couple of months, though, I think her opinion may have started to sink in. Recently, my father mentioned that maybe I should be entitled to the whole ball of wax."

"Did Amanda know that Philippa was pushing to cut her off?"

"Philippa told Amanda all right. On more than one occasion."

* * *

An hour later, Miles left the beach to spend some time shopping in Marigot.

"The plot thickens," Lynne said once he was out of earshot.

"You're so flip, Mother," Damon chastised. "Which plot are you referring to?"

Lynne pushed her sunglasses onto her forehead. "Which plot? Amanda told you Raymond was in some sort of brig on the ship last night. But Miles claimed he was still on Saint Thomas."

"I don't understand why Miles lied," Damon said. "Why would he be embarrassed by something Raymond did?" He took a sip of beer.

"You're making a pretty big assumption." Lynne fanned herself with her Kindle. "It doesn't work quite as well as a book." She snickered.

"What assumption?" Damon asked.

"That Miles is lying."

Damon tilted his head, confused.

"Why couldn't Amanda be the person who was lying?" Lynne asked.

Damon felt like he'd been punched in the stomach. "I hadn't even considered that. Why would Amanda tell me Raymond had been apprehended by security if he'd just missed the boat?"

"I have no idea. It's just an alternate theory."

The pair sat in silence for a minute. Finally, Damon said, "If Raymond was, in fact, stopped with a jar of spiders, there are two explanations I can think of. Either he set down his backpack and an islander mistook it for his own, or the 'business' Raymond told Vicky he had in Saint Thomas was to buy a bunch of spiders and smuggle them onto the ship."

"That sounds right," Lynne said. "But ship security must have released Raymond. Miles wouldn't have said he picked Raymond up by speedboat if he was still being held."

"True. Maybe security believed the jar had been put into his backpack by mistake."

Lynne nodded her agreement.

"But what if it wasn't a mistake?" Damon added. "Why would Raymond bring a jar of spiders onto a cruise ship?"

"To scare someone," Lynne ventured. Then her eyes widened. "To poison someone—were they tarantulas?"

Damon shook his head. "Amanda said they were only a half-inch long. That doesn't sound like a tarantula to me. But for all I know, there could be all kinds of poisonous spiders crawling around the Caribbean. The little ones might be the deadliest of the bunch."

"So do you think he could've been trying to poison someone?" Lynne asked.

"If he's a murderer, why not?"

"Raymond killed Philippa?"

"Honestly, Mother, I don't know."

The couple sat without speaking. Damon picked sand from between his toes.

"Miles seemed pretty chatty," Lynne said after several minutes as she applied sunscreen to her shoulders. "I'm actually a little surprised he sat down next to us."

"This stretch of beach isn't very crowded today," Damon said. "Ignoring us would've come across as antisocial."

"He could've just pretended he didn't see us."

"I suppose so. Perhaps he didn't see us simply by happenstance. Maybe he sought us out. He did just drop a motive for Amanda to kill Philippa into our laps like a ton of brinks."

"True. But we're not the police, and Philippa's death was ruled a suicide. Why put Amanda in our crosshairs?"

Damon shrugged and took a drink of his beer.

"If Philippa was murdered, do you think Amanda *could* have done it?" Lynne asked.

Damon sighed and looked down at his drink. "I suppose, especially if Philippa was almost to the point of getting Houston to redirect her share of the trust. The problem is that every other person in that family had a decent reason to do away with Philippa, too."

"Let's play this out," Lynne said and positioned her beach chair upright. Damon sensed she was starting to get as interested as he was. "There are seven family members," she said. "Do we have motives for all seven?"

Damon thought for a minute. "I can think of five or six, but some are stronger than others."

"Go ahead," Lynne said. "I'll pretend you've convinced me that Philippa was murdered."

"Thanks, Mother." Damon closed his eyes as he spoke. "Let's start at the top of the family. Houston's the only one I don't have a decent motive for, yet."

"Yet?"

"Yes. He was named in the suicide note—possibly because Philippa felt Houston was too stingy when it came to passing money along to her and Miles, even though Miles was a beneficiary of the trust and had been tapped for the CEO position. But that doesn't provide Houston with an incentive to murder Philippa. Then again, I don't have anything to exculpate Houston, so I haven't ruled him out yet."

"Okay. Who's next?" Lynne asked. "Kitty?"

"Sure," Damon said. "She didn't like Philippa because she wanted Miles to marry someone higher up the social food chain."

"If she didn't like the cards Philippa brought to the family table, why wait until now to do away with her? She and Miles had been married for over twenty years."

"I agree," Damon said. "For now, she's pretty low down on my list. Next is Miles. He's sleeping with Vicky. If he wanted to be with her but not get taken for a ride in a divorce proceeding or upset his conservative father, murdering Philippa in a way that looked like suicide would be one way to achieve his goal."

"I don't see how Ms. Frumpy Pants is a prize," Lynne countered, "but if I had to rank my list of suspects, I suppose Miles would be near the top. Especially given that he may be lying about what happened to Raymond yesterday."

"Okay, next is Amanda." Damon sat up and raked a hand through his thinning hair. "If Miles was honest about Philippa wanting to push Amanda off the family gravy train, as much as I hate to admit it, I think Amanda needs to be toward the top, too."

"Good." Lynne clapped her hands together. "Don't let personal preference bias you. Who's next? Candice?"

"You're getting into this, Mother," Damon teased.

"So what?" she challenged. "It's like an Agatha Christie book come to life. I see why you're so excited to get started on your police training."

"Excited, but nervous. As for Candice, her mother forced her to terminate her pregnancy against her will. But on the flip side, she's the only one who seemed genuinely saddened by Philippa's death. And she was in the ice box with Philippa's body and didn't take the 'meet me' note. I'd say that almost certainly rules her out."

"Agreed. Let's move on to the Carmichaels."

"Raymond first," Damon said. "Miles is sleeping with his wife and stole the grocery-chain client that would've given him a stake in Drummiller Box and Board. I'd say he had a tremendous motive to harm Miles. But why Philippa?"

Lynne pondered the question, digging her toes into the sand. "Could he have made a mistake?" she asked. "Maybe Raymond intended Miles to receive the 'meet me' note, but he put it under the wrong door."

Damon considered the proposition. "We don't know how the note was passed to Philippa. But if it was slipped under her stateroom door, he could've made a mistake—her room was right next to Miles's." Damon drank his Negra Modelo. "But if the note was intended for Miles, why kill Philippa when she showed up behind the aquatics theater?"

"Good point," Lynne said.

"Still, I'm not ready to cross Raymond off of my list. Especially if he tried to bring a jar of spiders on board—there's bound to be more to his story than we know."

"I agree. Last on the list is Vicky, and she's easy. Vicky's in love with Miles, and to land him, she decides to kill off Philippa, then divorce Raymond."

"Very clean and tidy."

"It would be nice to have a theory pan out," Lynne said with a wink. "Because my theory on inertia doesn't seem to be gaining any momentum."

Damon laughed. "The killer had to plant the suicide note in Philippa's nightstand," he said, changing gears. "Who would've had the most ready access to Philippa's stateroom?"

"The Drummillers and Carmichaels all came on board together," Lynne said. "Philippa could've let any one of them in."

"But if Philippa let the murderer inside, how could he plant the suicide note without her noticing—the staterooms are tiny."

"He—or she—waited until Philippa was in the bathroom?"

Damon didn't respond right away, his thoughts drifting to the wine-spilling maneuver he used to induce Amanda into her shower. After a moment, he said, "We're assuming that the murderer left the suicide note in Philippa's nightstand *before* she went overboard."

"Yes."

"Just imagine if Philippa had discovered it before she died!"

Lynne smiled. "That would have been one heck of a shock. But I don't see how the killer could've put the suicide note in her stateroom after the fact. The police found one of her SeaPass cards in her wet clothes, and the inspector found the other in her room."

"The murderer could've used it after he killed her, then left it on her dresser," Damon opined.

"How did he get the card in the first place?"

"Perhaps—"

"I have it," Lynne shouted. "The killer took Philippa's spare SeaPass card when she invited him inside her room earlier in the day."

Damon groaned. "No, no. The murderer only had to go into her room earlier in the day if he *didn't* have Philippa's extra card."

"Oh, right."

After a minute of silence, Damon smacked his head. "The killer was in Philippa's room before she died."

Lynne looked at him, clearly waiting for more.

"The suicide note was *under* the Bible when Inspector Albury found it."

"So?"

"The murderer put it underneath just in case Philippa opened her nightstand drawer. If we ask the Drummillers, I suspect we'd discover Philippa wasn't religious. So if she happened to open the drawer, she wouldn't pick up the Bible and see the note. But the killer would expect the police to search the room thoroughly and find it."

"I like that," Lynne said. "Plus, that definitely points to Philippa as a murder victim. I can see someone who commits suicide putting a note inside a drawer, but why hide it?"

"Okay, now we're getting somewhere," Damon said. "We think the murderer was in Philippa's room before she died to plant the suicide note. What about the 'meet me' note? I didn't notice whether Philippa was carrying a handbag. Did you?"

"I think she had a small clutch at the Crooner."

"With a snap?"

"Yes."

"That might be hard for someone to put a note into without being noticed. My guess is the killer slipped it under Philippa's door sometime before she went to bed."

"It could've been right after she went down to the Pelican Room for dinner on the first night. Too bad we got there after all of the Drummillers and Carmichaels—we don't know who arrived at the table after Philippa."

"I don't think that matters. Unless it was Miles, the murderer could've slipped the note under her door while we four were at the Crooner."

Chapter 14

Dinner in the Pelican Room was a stilted affair. Raymond appeared distant, and Miles was short-tempered.

"We missed you last night at dinner, Raymond," Jack said. "Did you get a better offer?" *Thank you, Jack.* Damon had been longing to ask Raymond where he'd spent the previous evening, but hadn't wanted to come off as impertinent given Miles's explanation earlier in the day.

Raymond looked down at a plate of speckled trout. "No," he said just above a whisper.

Miles and Houston exchanged glances, then Houston—staring intently at the other members of the Drummiller clan—said, "Raymond missed the boat last night. He got caught up shopping in Saint Thomas."

Damon spotted Amanda rolling her eyes in Houston's direction—a reaction he'd seen from Candice multiple times. *It must run in the family*, Damon thought.

"Well, that sounds downright absentminded," Jack said to Raymond. "Didn't you have a watch?"

Raymond bent his head lower—he looked as if he'd relish swapping places with the trout.

Fava laid a hand on Jack's arm. "He clearly doesn't want to talk about it," she said softly. "Let it go."

Jack patted her hand and smiled. "Well, Fava and I had quite a day, today, didn't we, dear?"

"We did," the beauty replied as Niels approached with a pitcher of water. "Jack bought me this gorgeous necklace." A large emerald-cut stone dangled from a delicate, gold chain that graced Fava's neck. The glitzy, blue gem was topped by an inverted triangle of three round diamonds. "I just love sapphires," Fava said with glee.

Kitty and Lynne gushed in obligatory fashion.

Damon glanced in Fava's direction. If she felt his eyes on her, she ignored them. Perhaps the necklace constituted payment for her complicity in Jack's scheme. Damon had passed the photos of Fava's finger to Captain Harris twenty-four hours earlier, and he longed to know whether the cruise line's attorneys had played hardball.

Candice, who had been visibly disgusted by Jack's plan to sue the cruise line, scowled. "Did you buy that necklace with the settlement money you intend to get for all of your *pain and suffering?*"

"Oh, that?" Jack replied with zest. "I decided to drop the claim." He scratched a withered cheek and mustered an air of self-assurance. "My attorney wasn't pleased. He knew the ship's crew had been negligent and wanted to go for the jugular. But not much harm was done. The inside of my mouth will be healed in another day or two, and I just didn't feel it was right to press on."

"Well, that was very decent of you," Candice muttered.

Jack rewarded her with a knavish smile.

Lynne squeezed Damon's knee under the table. From behind Jack, Niels gave Damon a wink and said a silent "thank you." Damon was thrilled. Despite Jack's rhetoric, Damon knew that his detective work, along with Lynne's photos, had thwarted the scheme.

Damon ventured a look in Fava's direction.

Silently, she mouthed, "well done," then turned away, fingering her new necklace.

* * *

After dinner, Damon and Lynne parted ways. Lynne was on her way to Shadow's Lounge to see Rudy Kent, the doctor from Boston. Damon took in a comedy production put on by the *Vitamin's* entertainment staff, then decided to check out Suede, a dance club.

Heavy base beats and pulsating lights jarred Damon's senses. For a nightclub, it was still early—before eleven o'clock. The dance floor was empty but for a pair of teenage girls in denim minis gyrating in unison. Damon approached the bar. At the far end, three boys were unsuccessfully trying to catch the girls' attention.

"It's too loud in here," Damon said to himself and turned to leave.

"For me too, my good man," a familiar voice replied.

Damon stopped and the man behind the bar, who had been polishing glasses with his face to the wall, spun around. It was the bartender from the crew bar, Disco.

"Poppy, right?" Damon said loudly.

"Yes sir, Mr. Police Officer Jackson," the clever young man replied.

Damon recalled the twenties he'd slipped Poppy. "I thought you were the crew's bartender."

"I'm filling in for a friend who's under the weather tonight. Not that I'm one to judge, sir, but don't you think you're a bit old for Suede?"

"I do," Damon shouted over the music. "This is the first time I've set foot in here. I didn't know it was an under-twenty-one club."

"The teenagers need some place to hang out."

"Makes sense," Damon said. "Can you do me a favor?"

The bartender laid the backs of his hands on the bar in a welcoming gesture.

"The next time you see Ricki, the girl from the kitchen staff I was with on Tuesday night, tell her she has nothing to worry about." Damon knew Niels would let Ricki know that Jack wasn't pursuing a legal claim, but Damon wanted to curry favor with Poppy.

Poppy gave Damon a roguish smile. "I'll do that," he said. "It sounds like you did Miss Ricki a little bitty favor. I like it when the police help good people. And Miss Ricki is good people."

Damon was too tickled by the praise to tell the bartender that he wasn't an actual police officer. Instead, he thanked Poppy and asked, "You wouldn't happen to know any of the security guards?"

Poppy frowned. "What did I tell you on Tuesday night? I know *everyone* who works on the *Vit-A-Min*. Who in particular are you looking for, Officer Jackson?"

Damon took the hint and laid a wrinkled twenty on the bar. "One of the guards who was working the x-ray scanner for reboarding yesterday in Saint Thomas."

Poppy slid the twenty off of the bar in a motion befitting a pickpocket. "I know all of the crew who work security, but I can't say offhand who was working which shifts yesterday. Tell you what, Officer Jackson. Maybe my friend who tends bar here will be sick again tomorrow night, say at around ten o'clock. I'll hook you up with a guard who was onboarding in Saint Thomas. Just make sure you come back as Officer Grant. Or better yet, Officer Franklin."

* * *

Friday, January 17

On the second-to-last full day of the cruise, the *Vitamin* was at sea.

"You were already asleep by the time I returned to the room last night," Lynne said. She and Damon were enjoying a buffet breakfast in the Galleon.

"A good night's sleep every once in a while does wonders for one's outlook on life." Damon bit into a once-crisp blueberry pancake now drenched in maple syrup.

"So are you and Amanda on the *outs*?"

"I don't think we were ever on the *ins*. We hadn't made plans for the night and never ran into one another. How about you—was Rudy Kent at Shadow's Lounge?"

"He was, with his daughter Emily and her husband. Their two kids were in the Fun-Zone for the evening."

"Nice family?"

"Yes. Emily and her husband, Lucho, live in western Massachusetts, near Worchester. Though Emily was a bit shaken up last night."

Damon wiped his mouth with a napkin. "Why's that?"

"Just before I arrived, there was an incident. Rudy, Emily, and Lucho had been there for about a half hour, sitting at a table near the back. Rudy and Lucho were smoking—it's a cigar bar. All of a sudden, the lights went out."

"And?"

"Someone tried to steal her necklace," Lynne said.

"Tried?"

"Yes. While the lights were out, Emily felt a tug at the back of her neck. She screamed. When the lights came on—about thirty seconds after the place went dark—her necklace was gone. But the thief must've dropped it because Emily found it lying on the floor right next to her. The chain was snapped, but otherwise, she said it looked fine."

"Did she see anyone running out of the lounge?"

"No. And none of them had been paying attention to the other patrons so they weren't sure whether anyone left while it was dark."

"I'm surprised they couldn't see, even with the lights off. Doesn't Shadow's Lounge overlook the promenade like the Crooner does?"

"No. Smoking's allowed so it's pretty isolated. Rudy said that when the lights went out, it was completely dark."

"Was the necklace valuable?"

"I didn't ask, but I assume so. Emily wasn't wearing it when I arrived at the lounge—nor could she with a snapped chain. I imagine she tucked it into the bottom of her handbag. Rudy told me it had been a recent anniversary present from her husband, and she'd worn it every night of the trip."

"Interesting," Damon said. "Who turned the lights back on?"

"One of the bartenders. Apparently, there's a set of switches near the cigar cases."

"So if the switches are in an area open to the public, either a passenger or a crew member could've killed the lights."

"I suppose that's right."

"Did Emily call ship security?"

"I don't think so—the manager of the lounge said he'd write up a report on the incident. Emily was frightened, but at least she still has her necklace. She'll just have to get the chain fixed back in Worchester."

"Well, I hope she's able enjoy the rest of the cruise," Damon said and focused on his pancakes.

"I'm sure she will. Emily struck me as a grounded and confident woman. You'll have the chance to meet her. Rudy invited us to dine with them tonight."

Damon looked up. "I didn't think we were allowed to move tables."

"In the formal dining rooms, we're not. But Rudy made a reservation at Braised." The steakhouse served as an alternative to the formal dining rooms, albeit one that came with an additional charge.

"Sounds like a welcome change," Damon said. "But if one of us sees a Drummiller or Carmichael today, we should let them know. Houston hasn't been pleased with the lack of a full table."

"We're not his *family*, Damon. But, yes, if either of us runs into one of them today, we can pass along our plans."

* * *

Midafternoon, Damon was relaxing in a hot tub in the spa area. He'd just finished receiving a hot-stones massage. The Relaxation Center was cool and the lights, dimmed. The sound of birds chirped from speakers above tall indoor plants—the place was a model of tranquility. Damon had the hot tub to himself and was enjoying the bubbling sensation when he heard his name.

He opened his eyes to see Kitty slowly descending the whirlpool's steps in a large-skirted bathing suit.

"Did you have a treatment, Mr. Lassard?" Kitty asked with a giggle that made her sound more like a schoolgirl than a woman who'd seen her seventieth birthday.

"Yes, a massage. How about you?"

"An oxygen facial." Another laugh.

Damon had no idea what that entailed but didn't dare probe. Instead, he asked, "Is Houston in the spa as well?"

Kitty guffawed. "No, he's in the gym with one of the ship's trainers. My dear Houston doesn't consider the spa to be a very manly place. Of course, I know for a fact he's had a manicure or two in his day."

The two passed several minutes in a silence, Damon trying to enjoy the calm atmosphere. He breathed in deeply and smelled alcohol. Was it coming from Kitty's pores? Then Damon recalled the dinner reservations Rudy Kent had made. "We won't be joining you for dinner tonight," he said. "We're going to Braised with someone my mother befriended and his family."

Kitty's eyes twinkled. "Good for her. It's nice to see a woman your mother's age who puts herself together well and can attract men." She looked down at her own body and frowned. "Not something I ever had the willpower to accomplish."

Damon didn't know how to respond.

Kitty took in his look of discomfort. "Oh, don't you worry about me. Houston doesn't have a wandering eye." She winked at him. "Besides, I think his natural urges slowed down years ago."

Damon looked toward his toes. They were obscured by bubbles.

"Though deviancy does-s-seem to run in the family," Kitty said, her words slurring together.

Damon realized the woman was completely smashed. "Did you have a few drinks with your facial, Kitty?" he asked.

"Nope! But I might have ordered a bottle of champagne with lunch." She burst out laughing, sending a rush of waves in Damon's direction.

Damon was about to make an excuse to leave when a thought struck him. Kitty was so drunk, her guard was likely down—a perfect time to ask some questions.

"You said 'deviancy runs in the family,' Kitty. Have there been a lot of problems with fidelity?" Damon asked in as breezy of a manner as he could muster.

"Just with Miles," Kitty replied without hesitation. "He's all but shacking up with Vicky right under Raymond's nose. Amanda, on the other hand, had what she described as an 'open marriage' with her ex-husband. They used to go to *swingers* parties together. I'm not sure if that counts as being unfaithful, but it's downright tawdry if you ask me. Last but not least is my poor, sweet Houston."

Damon waited as Kitty's wrinkled face contorted with a memory. "His own daughter-in-law," she nearly shouted. Kitty's face turned a bluish color as a hearty chortle turned quickly into a deep, throaty cough.

Damon opened his eyes with amazement. "Houston and Philippa?" he asked in disbelief.

Kitty took a moment to catch her breath. "Oh, it's not as bad as you think. Houston and I were separated at the time. And it happened before Philippa and Miles even started dating. She was Houston's secretary. How tediously cliché. Philippa—who still went by Jennifer back then—was quite a catch in the looks department, and I suspect she saw Houston as her golden ticket. Get the rich older man to drop his overweight, dried-up wife and marry her."

"I thought you were separated."

Kitty waived a hand. "Yes, we both needed a little time to find ourselves. But deep down I knew we'd get back together. We always had a lot of love between us. Of course, I don't doubt for a minute that Philippa had her eye on him six months earlier—from the day she set foot in that office."

"Was she the cause of the separation?"

Kitty laughed. "Goodness no. But she had the nerve to pretend she was sleeping with Houston before we split."

"How can you be sure they weren't?"

"I was close with one of Houston's accountants, and she knew everything that went on in the office."

"So Philippa must've known you knew about her fling with Houston."

Kitty snorted. "She sure did, after she tried to blackmail him a few years ago—demanded a king's ransom. When Houston told her I already knew and we'd been on a break at the time, she modified her tactics and claimed their affair had begun before we separated. Houston told her to pound sand. He wasn't paying a dime. She would have been better off threatening to tell Miles. He hasn't a clue."

Damon nodded his head, taking in the information. "So how did Philippa and Miles end up with each other?"

"Houston dropped her when we got back together. Philippa went straight from father to son." Kitty slurred the "s" in son. "Miles was still in his twenties and couldn't believe his luck when the fetching secretary started flirting with him. He had no idea she'd been with Houston. Philippa quit her job shortly after she and Miles began dating, and focused on reeling him in for the long haul. But make no mistake, Mr. Lassard, her end game all along was Houston's money. If you can't get the source, go to the next in line."

The story made sense to Damon—it aligned with Philippa making a play for Amanda's share of the Drummiller family trust. It also gave Kitty a second, and weightier, motive to kill Philippa: Revenge for sleeping with her husband. Kitty and Houston may have been separated, but it couldn't be easy for her to have Philippa around as a constant reminder of her husband's conquest.

And what about Miles? Had he found out about the decades-old relationship between his father and wife and murdered Philippa in outrage? Maybe not—on the beach in Saint Martin, Miles suspected the "Houston Drummiller can rot in hell" line derived from Philippa's anger over not getting hold of Amanda's share of Houston's wealth. More likely, it referenced her brief history with Houston. Miles, of course, could have been acting. Or he could've written the line on Philippa's suicide note himself without even knowing she'd slept with his father in an early attempt to lay claim to Houston's money.

Kitty had her eyes closed and was gently snoring. Damon closed his as well and allowed his mind to wander. If "Houston Drummiller can rot in hell" was directed at the family patriarch's former relationship with Philippa, who on board the *Vitamin* was aware of it? Houston and Kitty for certain. Not Miles if Kitty was being honest. That left Amanda, Candice, Raymond, and Vicky. If none of them knew of the fling, had Houston or Kitty inadvertently implicated himself—or herself—by writing that line in the suicide note?

Chapter 15

The interior of Braised reminded Damon of a cathedral, complete with faux parapets and flying buttresses. Dark wainscoting and ebony-colored tables gave the steakhouse a morose feel.

Despite the gloomy setting, two of Damon and Lynne's three dinner companions were delightful. Rudy Kent, an oral surgeon in his late fifties, had forearms that could've been sculpted in bronze. *Years of extractions,* Damon thought to himself. His daughter Emily had features of a classic beauty—almond-shaped eyes and high cheekbones—offset by the nose of a boxer who'd undergone repeated nasal-bridge repairs. The father-daughter duo was full of energy. Emily's husband, Lucho, who looked familiar to Damon, was uncomfortably reserved. Of South American descent, he had a neatly trimmed black beard and heavy eyebrows.

"Are your children in the Fun-Zone again tonight, Emily?" Lynne asked as drinks were served and a basket of Kalamata olive rolls was passed around the table.

"Yes," Emily said with a grin, leaning forward in the leather-backed booth. "That place is amazing. The kids have gone there for three or four hours every night, and they love it. Several other families drop off their children at the same time, so both Jacob and Sienna have made fast friends."

"It gives you and Lucho a nice break every day, too," Lynne observed.

"Total win-win." Emily spent the next fifteen minutes describing a host of Fun-Zone activities her children had enjoyed throughout the week.

Emily made the Fun-Zone sound so enticing, Damon almost wished he were there instead of at Braised, choosing his meal. In the end, he ordered conservatively—sirloin rather than a New York strip—because he suspected Rudy Kent would insist on paying for dinner.

"So, Damon, tell us about your ball-playing days in Japan," Rudy said, cutting into a slab of prime rib after their entrées had been served.

Damon described his stint with a Kyoto farm club and then his major-league career with the Hokkaido Nippon-Ham Fighters in Sapporo.

"That sounds incredibly exciting," Emily said. "Dad used to play a bit of baseball himself." She pointed to Rudy. "Nine months with the Phillies Triple-A team before he chucked it for med school."

Damon was impressed and told Rudy as much.

"It was fun, but I couldn't hit a Triple-A slider, let alone a Major League one. Though I once had three doubles in a single game." He lifted a tumbler of bourbon and winked at Lynne. "Unfortunately, the coach threw the bottle out before I had a chance for a fourth."

A chunk of glazed carrot caught in Damon's throat as he laughed, and he had to choke it down. Lynne's frame quaked.

"Oh, Daddy," Emily said and shook her head. Lucho didn't react. Instead, his eyes were focused on an unnaturally shaped piece of salmon on his plate.

"I heard you had quite a scare last night," Damon said to Emily. He stabbed at asparagus from a family-style bowl in the center of the table.

"I did." Emily put her hand to her throat. "Someone tried to steal my sapphire necklace. The chain snapped, but thankfully the thief didn't get away with it. Lucho had just given it to me for my birthday."

The neurons in Damon's brain fired. "It wasn't an emerald-cut sapphire, was it?"

Emily's eyelashes fluttered. "It was," she responded with a hint of astonishment. Then she turned to Lynne. "Oh, you must have told him."

Lynne shook her head. "I never saw the necklace."

Damon looked Emily in the eye. "Does it have a diamond cluster, too?"

Lucho spoke up. "I do not understand, Mr. Lassard. You know Emily's necklace?"

"I'm not sure," Damon said, thinking of the showpiece Fava was wearing around her neck the previous evening. "Do you have it with you, Emily?"

"It's in the safe in our stateroom," she said. "What are you getting at?"

"My son is a bit of a detective," Lynne said. "He's helped the police solve a couple of crimes back home. And he's joining the police force soon. Damon, you're thinking about Fava's necklace, right?"

Damon nodded.

"Who's Fava?" Rudy piped in.

"Let me explain," Damon said. He described Jack Jackman and his companion, then provided the details of Jack's incident with the glass shard. He gave his tablemates a blow-by-blow of his investigation.

"Last night, Jack told us that he'd changed his mind about pursuing legal action," Lynne said when Damon finished his story.

"Well done," Rudy chimed in.

"This is fascinating, Mr. Lassard," Lucho said. "But what does this have to do with my wife's necklace?"

"Last night at dinner," Damon said, "Fava was wearing an emerald-cut sapphire necklace with small diamonds. She said Jack bought it for her yesterday on Saint Martin."

Emily's eyebrows flew up.

"Your dinner seating is at six thirty, isn't it?" Rudy interjected.

"Yes," Lynne replied.

"And that's when you saw this Fava woman with the sapphire necklace?"

Lynne nodded.

"Then it must be a coincidence," Rudy concluded. "Emily's necklace was safely around her neck during *our* six thirty dinner seating last night."

"Plus, no one succeeded in stealing her necklace," Lucho added.

Damon considered the facts carefully as the conversation shifted and Lynne asked Rudy about his medical practice. In the middle of after-dinner coffee and port, Damon snapped his fingers.

All eyes turned to him. "I've seen that look before, Damon," Lynne said. "You're positively glowing. What is it?"

He focused his attention on Emily. "How closely did you look at your necklace after you found it on the floor last night?"

Emily squinted. "I don't really know. I was mainly focused on the broken chain."

"What about the gemstones—did they have any distinguishing characteristics?"

"Lucho just gave the necklace to me two weeks ago. I don't recall seeing any scratches or anything like that."

"It is flawless," Lucho said. "That sapphire was very expensive—$15,000."

Emily touched Lucho's forearm and smiled at him.

"What are you getting at, Damon?" Lynne asked.

"There's a jeweler on board the *Vitamin*, right?"

"Yes, Hector's," Lynne said. "On the promenade."

"Do you know how long it stays open?"

"Probably until ten," Lynne said. "Most of the shops are open until then."

Damon looked down at his watch. It was only 8:15. He was scheduled to meet Poppy and, he hoped, a member of the ship's security team at ten o'clock in Suede. "Emily, can you get your necklace so we can take it to Hector's?" he asked.

"Mr. Lassard!" Lucho bellowed. "Please tell us what you're talking about."

"He believes the necklace inside your stateroom safe is a fake," Rudy said, jumping back into the conversation. "Right, Damon?"

"Yes," Damon replied. "I think that Jack Jackman and Fava were upset that their insurance-fraud ploy didn't pan out, and they didn't want to leave the ship empty-handed. My mother told me you were wearing your new necklace all week—is that right, Emily?"

She nodded.

"Well, I think Jack and Fava noticed. One of the pair turned out the lights in the cigar bar while the other snatched your necklace and dropped a fake—which Fava had shown off at dinner—on the floor. That way, your distress would be minimal and the crew wouldn't feel obligated to launch a full-scale security sweep." He described Jack's and Fava's physical characteristics. "Did you see them in Shadow's Lounge?" Damon asked.

Both Rudy and Emily shrugged, but Lucho said, "They sound familiar. I can't be certain, but I may have seen them before the lights went out."

Damon tightened the grip around his fork. "Did you notice them after?"

"No, but I wasn't paying attention." Lucho paused. "Now that I think about it, I believe I've noticed them one or two other times on the ship."

"Maybe they were scouting you, Emily," Lynne said.

Emily shuddered, then stood. "I'll be back in ten minutes with the necklace."

As they waited for her to return, Damon sipped his coffee and considered his tablemates. Lucho, head down, was scooping forkfuls of Baked Alaska into his mouth. He'd placed a rush order for the dessert as soon as Emily left the table. Apparently she'd put him on a diet so Lucho had been sneaking desserts during the trip. Rudy Kent looked deep in thought.

"What's on your mind, Rudy?" Damon asked after a minute.

"I was just thinking about this situation. To be honest, I don't know that you're right."

Damon waited for him to continue.

"Here's the problem I have," Rudy said. "It does seem highly coincidental that this con artist Jackman bought his girlfriend a necklace just like Emily's hours before someone tried to steal it. But what I find even more implausible is how Jackman could've found a fake necklace identical to Emily's smack in the middle of the ocean."

"Saint Martin has a lot of jewelry stores," Lynne said. "I'm sure they have knock-off dealers, too."

"I have no doubt," Rudy agreed, "but we're not talking about a pair of diamond stud earrings. Emily's necklace looked fairly unique to me."

Damon's face grew hot. Rudy made an excellent point.

Lucho looked up from his dessert. "Perhaps the thieves had a false one made."

"Made?" Lynne asked.

"Why not? They see Emily wearing her expensive necklace every night. So they take a photograph of it. Use a zoom lens." Damon and Lynne looked at each other—it was the same method Lynne had used to document the cut on Fava's finger. "They get off of the ship in Saint Martin. Many locals are hanging around the port looking for rich cruise ship passengers. They offer taxi service, sell goods. We've all seen them. A local takes this Jack and Fava to a jewelry counterfeiter. They show him the picture on the camera screen. A few hours later they are back on the ship with a..." He searched for the right word.

"A replica," Damon offered.

"Yes, a replica."

Damon continued Lucho's line of thought. "Jack pays the counterfeiter a couple hundred bucks, then Fava shows us the replica at dinner on the off chance something goes wrong with the snatch-and-exchange. We're witnesses that she had it at six thirty."

"The thieves get a $15,000 necklace and leave a worthless fake on the floor," Lucho concluded. "Not bad for a day's work."

Minutes later, Emily returned, clutching a black, velvet necklace box. "Let's go," she said.

Rudy put dinner on his SeaPass card over Damon's protests, which earned the oral surgeon a peck on the cheek from Lynne. Then the group paraded to Hector's near the center of the *Vitamin's* promenade on the fifth deck.

The jewelry shop was empty but for a sleekly dressed blond saleswoman behind the counter and, to her side, an older man in a rumpled suit. He was crunching numbers at a calculator the size of a laptop computer.

"Just browsing or can I help you find something in particular?" the blonde asked as Damon's group entered.

Emily stepped toward her. "Actually, we're hoping that someone could take a look at my necklace." She held out the black box.

"Our man Gustavo can fix most anything," the saleswoman said. "But he won't be in until tomorrow morning. If you leave it with me, I can call your stateroom with a quote after he's taken a look."

Emily raised a hand. "The necklace doesn't need to be fixed…. Actually it does, but that's not why I brought it here. Is there any chance you could tell me whether the sapphire is real."

The disheveled-looking man raised his head. "I'm Vide Adalsteinn, the manager. Perhaps I could have a look?" He reached across the counter, and Emily handed him the box.

After retrieving a gem microscope from a back room, Vide snapped open the case and removed a stunning necklace. Damon's eyes widened to saucers— it was different than Fava's. The primary gemstone was an emerald-cut sapphire, but Emily's was in a horizontal position while Fava's was vertical. And Fava's had an inverted triangle of three diamonds perched at its apex while the six small stones on Emily's were shaped in a rectangle along the top edge of the sapphire. Damon opened his mouth to stop the proceeding, but something inside held him back. He swept his head around to catch his mother's attention, but she was busy studying bracelets with Rudy.

After twenty seconds of examination, Vide looked up from the microscope at Emily. "I'm sorry to tell you, ma'am, but what you have here is blue tourmaline, not sapphire. And the diamonds aren't real either. The whole piece is worth $150 American, $200 tops."

Emily's jaw dropped. Lucho's face reddened to a shade of burgundy. "You show me this Jack Jackman," he exploded in Damon's direction.

Damon was about to explain that Fava's necklace was different when Lynne stepped over and peered down at the piece. She looked from Damon to Lucho.

"This necklace looks identical to the one you bought Emily for her birthday?" she queried.

"Yes, it is the same," Lucho said. "What are the words? Spitting image. Only the one I bought cost much more."

"Don't you think you should speak with security rather than Mr. Jackman?" Lynne asked.

"No need for security." Lucho grunted. "Just point out to me this Jackman fellow, and I'll handle him directly."

"The only time and place I know he'll be for certain," Lynne replied, "is at our dining table in the Pelican Room tomorrow night. It's the last dinner of the cruise, so if you come by to say hello, I can point him out to you."

"That would be satisfactory," Lucho said to Lynne. "Thank you." He unclenched his fingers, which had curled into a fist.

Lynne described the location of their table to Lucho, then made plans with Rudy to meet poolside in the morning. Emily thanked Vide for his time, slipped the counterfeit necklace into her case, and left Hector's with her father and husband.

Damon and Lynne went in the opposite direction, making their way to their stateroom. Once safely inside, Damon asked, "What are you up to? We both know Emily's necklace is different than Fava's."

"I want to see Lucho and Jack duke it out like men," she retorted.

Damon stepped into the bathroom to change from his jacket and tie into more comfortable clothing. "Seriously," he said through the door. "What gives?"

"You didn't speak up either. Why not?"

"I don't know. But something seemed off."

"Exactly," Lynne said. "And it turns out something *is* off. I think there's some sort of trickery going on, but Jack and Fava have nothing to do with it."

"Someone *else* snapped a photo of Emily's necklace and had a forgery made?" Damon slipped on jeans then examined his tan in the bathroom mirror.

"No. I'm not sure there was a counterfeiter *on Saint Martin.*"

"There has to be one," Damon protested. "The necklace Emily picked up off of the floor was a fake."

"Yes, I know that. But how do we know a thief ripped it from her throat?"

Damon opened the bathroom door, walked across the stateroom, and plopped down on the pull-out sofa bed. He checked his watch—he had to meet Poppy in fifteen minutes. "You think Rudy and his family are up to something?" Damon asked with disbelief.

"Not Rudy and not the whole family," Lynne said. "Just Lucho."

"Lucho?" Damon repeated. "He seemed pretty upset about the theft."

"To me, his change in manner after dinner seemed strange," Lynne said, sitting on the bed and tucking her feet under her backside. "All meal long, the man hardly says two words. But when the conversation came around to Emily's necklace and the possibility that it had been snatched by Jack or Fava, Lucho latched on. He seemed determined to make the pieces of the story fit."

"You're right, now that I think about it. But what does it mean? Why would Lucho want to pin a jewel theft on two people he doesn't know?"

"To avert attention from himself, of course," Lynne said. "I think he had a counterfeit necklace made before he ever boarded the ship. He pulls the stunt in the cigar bar and recovers fifteen thousand from his insurance company. That fifteen grand covers his cost for the original necklace, only he still has the original. I bet it's hidden in his stateroom right now."

"Ugh, more insurance fraud," Damon said. "So then what? He sells the real necklace at a pawn shop?"

"Why not? If he can net two-thirds of its value, that's a cool ten thousand in his pocket."

"So why would he want to confront Jack Jackman?" Damon asked.

"He doesn't," Lynne replied. "My guess is he'll pull Jack aside and talk with him in private about something completely unrelated, then tell Rudy and Emily that Jack denied the whole thing."

"You don't think Rudy or Emily will press him to go to the police?"

"I doubt Rudy would—he doesn't seem the type to butt into his daughter's affairs unless absolutely necessary. I'm not so sure about Emily, but I suspect the insurance company will need to see a police report before paying out the claim. Lucho will probably insist on handling it and just won't mention Jack."

Damon thought for a moment, then said, "Even if I hadn't suggested that Emily get the sapphire inspected by an expert, I suppose Lucho would've come up with a plan to do it. Otherwise, he'd have no way of *finding out* that the necklace was a fake."

"Maybe, maybe not. If Emily wasn't suspicious, Lucho could have let her go along believing the necklace was real—no need to even tell her about the insurance claim unless she ever saw the paperwork. On the other hand, I also could see him coming home from work one day, necklace in hand. *'Honey, I got the chain fixed on your new necklace, but I have some bad news. I took it to the same jeweler I bought it from, and he said something didn't look quite right. So he used one of those microscopes to take a closer look. Turns out you were robbed on the ship.'* Either way, he'd get away scot-free."

"So you really think Lucho ripped the necklace from his own wife's neck?"

"I do," Lynne said.

That makes sense, Damon thought. But... "Wait a minute. Lucho was sitting with Rudy and Emily when the lights went out, right?"

"I believe so. Oh... If Lucho pulled a yank-and-switch on Emily, who turned out the lights?"

"Exactly." Damon rose to leave. "I have to meet someone. I'm fishing for information about Raymond's whereabouts the other night. What's your plan for the conniving Lucho?"

"What makes you think I have a plan?"

"You've been quite proactive on this trip—tipping off Jack that I was suspicious of his charade, then taking those pictures of Fava's finger."

Lynne smiled. "I don't know what to do about Lucho yet. I need time to think. You concentrate on Raymond, and we'll compare notes later tonight. Or first thing in the morning if you get back late. We only have one more full day on board. If Philippa Drummiller was murdered, you need to shake things loose. And quickly."

Chapter 16

A thudding beat pumping from enormous speakers assaulted Damon when he entered Suede. A group of ten middle-schoolers stood on the dance floor, bobbing their heads in time with the beat. Beyond them, Poppy stood behind the bar, waving. Damon headed Poppy's way, unable to keep his eyes off a fish tank the size of a big-screen television that formed the center of a shelving unit lined with bottles of nonalcoholic beverages.

Poppy followed Damon's gaze to the aquarium. "Two fish are in a tank," the bartender said. "One says to the other, 'you man the guns, I'll drive.'"

Damon laughed. "I see your friend was sick again tonight."

"Yes, though he's scheduled to make a miraculous recovery in fifteen minutes so he can relieve me. I'm glad you got here on time. Joaquin has a shift starting at ten thirty."

"He's a security guard?" Damon asked. He removed a pair of one hundred dollar bills from his pocket and set them on the bar.

"Yes. He's in back. Give me a second." Poppy left Damon and the bills alone.

A moment later, the bartender returned with a barrel-chested Hispanic who had muscles bulging from beneath his crew-cut T-shirt. "Joaquin was at the onboarding station in Saint Thomas on Wednesday," Poppy said by way of introduction. He slid the hundreds off of the bar and slipped one into Joaquin's palm. He pocketed the other and went to chat with two middle-aged women at the far end of the bar—probably chaperones of the kids on the dance floor.

"Poppy tells me you're a police officer," Joaquin said.

"Something like that," Damon responded.

Joaquin narrowed his eyes. "So what do you want to know about the Saint Thomas stop?"

"Did security apprehend a passenger named Raymond Carmichael?"

"We did."

Damon mentally checked a box—both Miles and Houston had lied about Raymond's whereabouts. "You were there?" he asked.

"Yes. I helped Yuniel, the guard who spotted the contraband, transport Mr. Carmichael to our confinement unit. It's next to the ship's security office."

"And he was held on the ship overnight?"

"The head of security released him at around midnight."

"What contraband did Mr. Carmichael board the ship with?" Damon asked.

"Spiders. Redbacks. Indigenous to Australia, I believe."

"Australia?"

"That's what Wikipedia says. The spiders were black, each with a red stripe on its back, so I did a little digging online."

"Are they dangerous?" Damon asked.

"You bet. They're a cousin to the black widow. A bite could be deadly, but there was an anti-venom developed in the 1950s."

I wonder how quickly a person bitten by a redback would have to get treated, Damon thought. By the time a victim was properly diagnosed, would there be time to save him? It could be a close call, especially if an anti-venom had to be shipped from Australia to a boat in the middle of the Caribbean.

"Any idea what Australian spiders were doing on Saint Thomas?" Damon asked, drumming his fingers on the bar.

"I don't, but you'd be surprised at what you can find on some of these islands."

"How many spiders were there?"

"Five. Inside a small pickle jar. Mr. Carmichael claimed he'd never seen them before."

"Do you believe him?"

"It doesn't matter what I believe. Mr. Thompson calls the shots. He's the head of security on the *Vitamin*."

"He let Raymond go, so he must have believed his story," Damon ventured cautiously.

"Maybe," Joaquin responded.

"You don't buy it?"

Joaquin appraised Damon silently.

Damon reached for his wallet and put another fifty dollars on the bar. Joaquin snapped it up. "I don't buy Mr. Carmichael's bullshit story at all," he said. "Someone put a horde of venomous spiders in his backpack by mistake? No way that happens. Mr. Thompson didn't believe the story, either."

Damon arched his eyebrows. "You know that?"

"That's what Yuniel said. He was in the security office with Mr. Thompson on Wednesday night."

"So if no one believed Raymond Carmichael, why did security release him?"

"Yuniel said Mr. Thompson was pressured into it by someone named Drummiller. Older man who has diamond-level status on the ship. He bullied Mr. Thompson and the captain into letting Mr. Carmichael go. He threatened lawsuits and a negative publicity campaign."

Damon thought for a moment. "Do you have any idea why a passenger would bring a jarful of poisonous spiders aboard the ship?"

"In my opinion, there's only one reason to have those redbacks, sir. To use the venom."

* * *

Damon wandered about the ship for a solid hour. He was looking for anyone in the Drummiller-Carmichael clan he could corner. Not that he had an angle to pursue. But at eleven o'clock on a Friday night, there was a good chance that alcohol could cloud better judgment, as it had with Kitty in the spa.

After striking out in the casino, the Irish pub, Foxtrot, the Crooner, Shadow's Lounge, and two other bars, Damon made his way up to the pool deck. A reggae band was entertaining at a poolside party. Damon spotted Raymond almost immediately. He was dressed in a gaudy Hawaiian shirt, sitting upright on a deck chair with a plate of pulled pork in his lap.

As Damon approached, Raymond smiled, showing off the gap between his front teeth, and pointed to an open chair to his right. Damon sat and said, "Nice evening for a pool party."

"That's for sure," Raymond replied. A day's worth of stubble dotted his chin.

A waiter approached and each of the men purchased a drink—a cocktail for Damon and club soda for Raymond. Unfortunately for Damon, Raymond was as sober as a priest on Sunday.

"Is Vicky here with you?" Damon asked.

"With me?" Raymond snorted. "No. Have you ever been married?"

"I haven't."

"I recommend you keep it that way."

Damon seized the opening. "Problems with Vicky?"

"That's an understatement. Maybe I should push her into committing suicide like good ol' Miles did with Philippa."

Wow, that's cold.

The waiter returned with their drinks. Once he withdrew, Damon said, "You think Miles prompted Philippa to kill herself?"

Raymond laughed. He sounded congested. "Did he tell her to throw herself overboard? No, I doubt that. But Miles is a Grade A jerk. I'm sure day-to-day life provided plenty of impetus."

Damon sipped his whiskey and ginger ale. Quietly, he said, "Houston and Kitty told me that Miles stole your grocery-chain client ten years ago."

Raymond's face squirreled up into a question mark. "They told you?" he huffed. "I'm sure Houston said I couldn't seal the deal."

Damon nodded.

"He's full of it. I was well on my way to locking them up, until Miles swooped in and gave the head of operations a big fat envelope under the table."

Damon took a deep breath. "Miles paid someone off to have the chain sign with him instead of you?"

"I couldn't prove it in a court of law, but I'm sure that's what happened," Raymond said, his face reddening. "I have no doubt."

"Did you tell Houston?" Damon asked.

"Of course, but he didn't want to hear it. 'I don't care how the sausage is made.' That's always been Houston's mantra."

"It sounds as if Houston isn't opposed to skirting the law. Is that how he built up Drummiller Box and Board?"

Raymond stared at Damon for a good ten seconds. "You sound like an undercover cop."

Damon shrugged his shoulders and took a drink. "Sorry. I didn't mean to pry. I just find family histories tremendously interesting."

"Especially when it's not your own family, right?" Raymond snickered.

Damon laughed. "That's for sure."

After a moment, Raymond said, "I worked with Houston for ten years, and I didn't see anyone acting particularly crooked. Houston's more ruthless than anything. He tells people that his longtime partner wanted to retire early. But Houston drove him out—he paid Zach Bristol a good price for his shares and never considered taking on another partner. He wanted control. It's the same reason he didn't replace Ernie."

Damon looked at Raymond with curiosity. "Who's he?"

"Ernie Mencken. He was one of Houston's original partners. Houston, Zach, and Ernie started the box-making business together, close to forty years ago."

"Did Houston buy out Ernie's interest, too?"

"No, no. Ernie died in a fire.... Just like my father."

Damon's mind raced in a hundred directions. Outwardly, he sipped his drink with forced patience, waiting for Raymond to continue.

"If I remember correctly, the cardboard plant caught fire when Miles and I were about ten years old." Raymond scowled. "Vicky told me that Houston went on the other night about how slipshod my father and grandfather were for not having sprinklers in the pharmacy or insurance on the place. That pisses me off—Houston's own partner died in a fire at *his* factory because *their* sprinklers malfunctioned." He shook his head, then mumbled, "At least Houston and Zach were lucky enough to have insurance."

"What happened to Ernie's share of the company?"

"I'm pretty sure Houston and Zach bought out Ernie's widow," Raymond said.

The reggae band changed tune—a lively offering that prompted passengers to dance on the deck. Raymond slumped back in his chair and closed his eyes.

Damon summoned the courage to posit the question eating away at him. "So, Raymond, why the redback spiders?"

Raymond jerked up. "What?"

"The spiders you acquired in Saint Thomas."

"I have no idea what you're talking about," Raymond said. His thin lips twisted.

"Come on, I know for a fact you didn't miss the ship in Saint Thomas. You were locked in a room next to the security office. You tried to bring a jar full of poisonous redback spiders on board."

Raymond paused in thought, presumably weighing his options. Finally, he said, "I didn't miss the boat, but someone put the spiders in my backpack. I set it on the ground next to one of those big blue mailboxes in town while I used a public restroom. I didn't think to check inside when I picked it back up."

"You left your backpack unattended in the streets of Charlotte Amalie?"

"Sure. I wasn't going to take it into the bathroom. I put my passport in the pocket of my shorts just in case someone decided to steal the bag."

"You didn't see the jar when you put your passport back inside your pack?" Damon asked with disbelief.

Raymond pulled his eyes away from Damon's stare. "I put it into a different pouch," he said feebly. "The backpack has three different compartments."

Damon pressed on. "Okay, but still, didn't you notice a difference in weight when you picked it up?"

"I've had enough of this conversation," Raymond said and stood.

"So you planned to let the redbacks loose in Miles's room?" Damon guessed.

Raymond glared at him. "Miles might be sleeping with my wife, but that doesn't..."

Damon couldn't stop himself from taking another jab. "He stole your grocery-chain client, too."

Raymond took a deep breath and stared up at the night sky. It was littered with stars. "I despise the man. Is that what you wanted to hear?"

Damon waited a moment. He hoped he hadn't miscalculated and grossly crossed the line with his accusation. But instead of apologizing, he asked, "So why did you agree to come on this cruise?" When Raymond didn't answer, Damon tried again. "You told Vicky you had business to attend to in Saint Thomas. You're telling me that had nothing to do with buying a jarful of spiders?"

Raymond turned to leave, then stopped and looked back at Damon. The whites of his eyes glowed red with fire, but his expression dripped with guilt. "I came because I wanted to spend time with my godmother. Besides, Houston was footing the bill." He stomped off in a huff.

* * *

"Shouldn't you be romping around in bed with Amanda?"

Damon had been thinking, eyes closed, on the poolside chair. The reggae band was taking a break, replaced by an audio recording featuring light instrumentals. Damon opened an eye at the sound of Candice's voice. She sat on the edge of the pool chair vacated by Raymond ten minutes earlier. Candice wore a tight, black-leather skirt riding up from her knees paired with a candy-apple red lace top.

"I haven't seen your aunt tonight," Damon said. "How was dinner?"

"Boring. As usual. At least Fava was there—she's a trip."

"How so?" Damon asked as he sat up.

"I don't understand her. She's only ten years older than me and she's here with someone my grandfather's age. It's so … gross." Candice sipped a mauve-colored drink through a straw shaped into a curlicue.

"I think he pays her bills back in Texas," Damon replied. He had no qualms about passing Fava's story along to Candice. *If it was even true,* Damon thought. Fava was a first-class liar and con artist. For all he knew, she could be Jack's granddaughter rather than his lover. He'd never seen them do more than touch hands and kiss each other on the cheek.

"Well, I suppose she can wait until he dies and hope he leaves everything to her," Candice said. "Not a whole lot different than why my mother married Daddy, I suppose—to get to Grandfather's money."

It was amazing to Damon how frankly and uniformly the Drummillers denigrated Philippa. Only days earlier, Candice was weeping over the loss of her mother. "I'm sure your mother wanted Houston to live a nice, long life," Damon said.

"Ha! That's rich. You didn't know *Philippa* at all. Deep down I loved her, but you should have seen her last year when Grandfather recovered. You could read the disappointment on her face—she was so transparent."

"Recovered?" Damon asked and sipped the melted ice at the bottom of his glass.

"He had colon cancer." Candice shrugged. "At first, the doctors didn't think it would be a big deal—they put him on chemo to shrink the tumor, and planned to remove it during surgery. But while he was under the knife, the surgeons found some abnormalities and couldn't get it all out."

"But he fully recovered?"

"Eventually, yes. The doctors treated him aggressively and ultimately rid his body of the cancer, but for about a week, things were looking pretty grim."

"Wow. It sounds like Houston was extremely lucky."

"He was, thank goodness." Candice stood. "If you want the room tonight with Amanda, it's all yours. I'm meeting up with some people at one of the clubs, and I doubt I'll be back before morning."

The reggae band started again after Candice departed. Damon sank back into his chair, closed his eyes again, and processed the new information. Colon cancer had Houston teetering on the verge of death. Surely the whole family had known of his medical condition.

So what? Damon already knew that Philippa had wanted Houston's money sooner rather than later. But it wasn't Houston's body in the ice box, it was Philippa's. *So why Philippa and why now?*

A waiter interrupted Damon's thoughts. He declined another drink. His mind was spinning and he wanted to stay sharp.

As he focused on the band's drummer pounding away, a new thought formed. Houston spent a week on his deathbed before recovering. What better way to pass one's final days than by cleansing your soul of guilt? Had Houston made a confession to Philippa that he regretted after recovering—a confession so dangerous that he had to kill her?

Chapter 17

Damon knocked on Amanda's stateroom door. It was just past midnight. For all Damon knew, she was asleep. Or inside with another man.

Amanda cracked open the door. Heavy, white cream pancaked her face. "Damon," she said with a note of surprise. "I missed you at dinner tonight. Do you want to come in?"

Damon stepped inside and Amanda excused herself to wash the mask from her face. "My mother made dinner plans for us at Braised with a man she met and his family," Damon explained.

"I heard," Amanda replied over the sound of running water. "Kitty told us at dinner."

I'm surprised she remembered, given her drunken condition, Damon thought. In the back of his mind, he'd hoped to find Amanda in an inebriated state. Not so he could bed her—he'd proven he didn't need to stack the deck for that—but to loosen her lips. If Houston had made a deathbed confession to Philippa, or anyone else in the family, Damon wanted to find out what was said.

Amanda exited the bathroom with glowing cheeks. "Do you want to go get a glass of wine?" she asked. "Or maybe you just came to fool around a little." She was dressed in pink-striped pajama pants and a black tank top.

"Neither right now. I was hoping to talk with you about something a little more serious." Damon sat on the edge of the bed.

Amanda jumped in beside him. Lying down, she sank an elbow into the comforter and propped her head in her hand. "Serious, huh? Don't ask me to marry you, Damon Lassard."

Damon laughed nervously. He turned to face her. "Nothing like that. I want to ask you something about your father."

"Okay," Amanda said cautiously. "Shoot." She sat up against the bed's headboard, her legs outstretched, ankles crossed.

"Candice told me that Houston had colon cancer last year. The doctors were able to get rid of it, but for a week or so things were dire."

"That about sums it up." Amanda tickled Damon's ribs with a toe. "Not an easy time for us."

Damon playfully swatted her foot away, then took a deep breath. "Amanda, when your father thought he was going to die, did he say anything to Philippa or anyone else in the family? Something he may have regretted after he recovered?"

Amanda cocked her head. "That's a very strange question. Why would you ask me that?"

"I'm just curious," Damon responded a bit too quickly.

Amanda pinched her lips together, and her chocolate eyes took on an icy hue. "Damon, what the hell is going on?"

Damon took a shot in the dark. "I don't know all of the details, but I heard he made a confession that rocked your whole family."

"Who told you that?" Amanda's upper lip arched into a fiendish smile.

"Candice," Damon lied.

"And what did my niece tell you?"

Damon was trapped. He hesitated, thinking.

Amanda drummed her fingers against her thigh. "I'm waiting."

He formulated the best guess he could muster. "Candice told me she's Houston's daughter, not Miles's."

"What?" Amanda shouted. "That's disgusting!" She sprang forward, her face inches from Damon's. "Candice told you..." She paused. "Candice thinks she's my sister?"

Before Damon could respond, Amanda jumped off of the bed and pulled a pair of Capri pants out of a drawer.

"Where are you going?" Damon stammered.

"To find Candice, that's where. Or better yet, my father. Wait, is Kitty her mother? Don't tell me it's more twisted than that!"

Damon couldn't let Amanda's agony go on. He held up his hands. "Wait. Candice didn't really tell me that."

Amanda threw the pants to the floor. "Now you're lying to me? Damon, none of this makes sense, and I think you better leave." She pointed to the door.

"Let me explain," Damon pleaded, refusing to stand.

"Explain what—that you have a sick fascination with other people's lives? With my family? What in the world are you trying to accomplish?"

Damon took a deep breath and folded his hands in his lap. "Let me be completely honest with you."

"That would be nice." She leaned back against the room's dresser and flipped a swath of dark-brown hair from her eyes.

"Back home, I've helped the police solve a couple of murder cases. Based on my experience and what I've seen on board the *Vitamin*, I don't think Philippa committed suicide." He looked her in the eyes. "I think she was murdered."

Damon's knees pulsated as he waited for Amanda's reaction. He knew he was taking a risk by pouring out his suspicions to a suspect.

"Murdered?" Amanda said incredulously, but Damon could sense she was concentrating. "But she wrote a suicide note."

"There was another note, too." Damon described the "meet me" note he'd found in Philippa's belongings.

Amanda took in the information without comment, then said, "Philippa was caustic to everyone. It wouldn't surprise me if she insulted someone after boarding the ship. But what could she have said that would cause a perfect stranger to kill her?"

"It may not have been a stranger," Damon said slowly.

Amanda's eyes widened. "You think one of us did it."

"That would make the most sense."

"We may not be a family of saints, but we're not—" Amanda's face grew pale.

"What is it?" Damon asked.

"Nothing." She opened the mini bar, uncapped a bottle of water, and took a long swallow.

"Amanda, did your father say something to the family when he thought he was dying?" It was just a hunch, but Damon couldn't let the point go.

Amanda stared at him without saying a word.

Damon kept his own mouth shut, intent on waiting her out.

After another minute, Amanda sighed. "He did. To me, Miles, and Philippa. Kitty was there, too, though she acted as if she already knew."

Damon wrinkled his eyebrows but stayed silent.

"But it wasn't anything he did," Amanda said defensively. "Just something he saw."

"What did he see?"

"It don't know why it matters. It can't possibly be related to Philippa's death—it has nothing to do with her."

"It could still be important," Damon said. "You can trust me."

Amanda sat on the bed, inches from Damon. "Daddy started his business with two partners," she said. "That was nearly forty years ago. Before I was even born. Daddy bought out Zach Bristol fifteen years ago, but there was another partner in the beginning."

"Ernie Mencken," Damon said.

"You've certainly been doing your homework." Amanda smiled. "About five years after they started the business, their cardboard plant caught fire. It was the only one they had at the time, near Rocky Mount. That's where Miles and I grew up."

"I heard that Ernie died in the fire."

Amanda looked down at the floor. "That's true. Or at least that's what Kitty and Daddy always told us."

"He didn't die?"

"No, he did." She took a sip of water, then said, "Daddy gathered us all together in his hospital room one evening, before the doctors were able to get his cancer under control. I think it was a Tuesday. Candice wasn't there—she'd come down from college to see him the prior weekend but had gone back to school. We all knew about the fire and that Ernie didn't make it out alive. But, lying there, Daddy admitted that he, Zach, and Ernie burned down the plant on purpose."

Damon nodded, silently urging Amanda to continue.

"According to Daddy, back then, they only had one large account, an electronics chain. These were early days, before the business really took off. Daddy said he and Zach found out that Ernie had been stealing from the client."

"Stealing?"

"Ernie was falsifying the records and charging the client for more cardboard product than was being manufactured and shipped."

"Wouldn't the company know how many boxes it was receiving?" Damon asked.

"I asked Daddy that very question," Amanda replied. "He said they shipped corrugated cardboard to facilities all over the mid-Atlantic and South for this chain and several of their subsidiaries and partners. Back then, without computer-tracking systems, it wasn't as easy to follow product shipments. Even so, Daddy said that the president of the electronics company had grown suspicious and demanded to review their books. Before the client had the chance to hire an auditor, my father and Zach conducted their own probe—up until then Ernie handled all of the finances. They discovered that he was cheating the client and keeping the money he skimmed for himself."

"So they decided to light a match?"

"Yes. Daddy and Zach confronted Ernie, and after a healthy bit of pressure—or cajoling as Daddy called it—he admitted he'd been cooking the books. There were no computers, just ledgers and paper files, which were all in Ernie's office. Daddy said the timing couldn't have been worse—he had two large companies he was about to land as clients. So if the auditor found the discrepancies, not only would Daddy and his partners lose the electronics chain, but they'd be discredited, and the new companies wouldn't sign on with them either. Daddy's company had insurance, so the three of them agreed to burn down the plant along with all of its files. Even if they wound up losing their first client, they'd rebuild with the insurance money and have the two new clients to start over with, bigger and better." Amanda plucked an elastic band from the nightstand and wound her hair into a ponytail. "Daddy said setting the fire never bothered his conscience. What gave him nightmares is what he saw Zach do to Ernie."

Damon leaned in close to Amanda. "What did Zach do?" he breathed.

"He…" Amanda shook her head. "It's just awful." A tear trickled down her cheek. "The three of them, Daddy, Zach, and Ernie, waited until all of the floor staff had gone home for the night. Apparently, Zach had researched how to make a fire look like it was caused by faulty wiring, and they turned off the sprinkler system. When they had the set-up ready, Zach asked Daddy to get the matches—he said he left them in a desk drawer in his office, which was on the opposite side of the plant from where they were lighting the fire. Daddy told us he thought Zach was acting a little strangely, so after he walked off in the direction of the offices, he hid behind a corner to spy on Zach and Ernie. Daddy saw Zach knock Ernie unconscious with a brick to the back of the head." Amanda wiped away a tear with the back of her hand. "Then Zach dragged Ernie into a supply room. Punishment for stealing, I suppose. Daddy got the matches and brought them back. He didn't say a word about what he'd seen. That's why Daddy felt so guilty—he knew Zach was murdering Ernie and did nothing to stop it. If he had, Ernie would've gone to the police, and Zach to jail. Their two new clients would have disappeared, as would Daddy's dream of a family fortune. And there was nothing more important to Daddy than building that fortune."

"So Ernie was unconscious and unable to escape the fire."

Amanda nodded. "Before they torched the plant, Zach told Daddy that Ernie didn't have the stomach to watch it burn so he'd gone home."

"Wasn't his car in the parking lot?" Damon asked.

"Miles asked Daddy that. Apparently, Ernie lived less than a mile away and walked to work when the weather was nice, as it had been that day."

Damon turned away from Amanda and sat in silence, thinking. He could finally visualize the events leading to Philippa's death with clarity.

"Damon," Amanda pleaded, interrupting his thoughts. "You can't tell anyone. I don't even know if Zach Bristol is still alive. If he is, I wouldn't care if he went to jail, but I couldn't bear to see anything happen to Daddy."

Damon didn't reply. He wouldn't pledge to keep any criminal activity a secret. There was no statute of limitations on murder; he wasn't so sure about insurance fraud. "I have to think through everything, Amanda," he said finally.

* * *

Five minutes later, Damon was back in his own stateroom.

Lynne rustled under her blanket. "Damon, is that you?"

"Yes," he whispered. "Sorry if the lights woke you."

Eyes still closed, Lynne murmured, "Find out anything?"

As he changed into his pajamas, Damon first relayed the substance of his conversation with Raymond about the spiders.

"It sounds like he wanted to poison Miles," Lynne said. "Maybe just to paralyze him. I suppose Houston and Miles decided to hush it up. Create a bogus story about him missing the boat and demand that the captain not take the matter any further."

"For the sake of the Drummiller name?"

"Nothing says scandal like one godbrother siccing venomous insects on another."

"Well, they'll still have to contend with the media's accounts of Philippa's *suicide* when they get home," Damon said and crawled into the sleeper sofa.

"Don't be so sure of that," Lynne countered. "I wouldn't be surprised if there's nothing more than an obituary in a local paper saying she died of a sudden illness contracted overseas."

Damon conceded the point, then summarized the story behind the demise of Ernie Mencken.

"So how does his death relate to Philippa's?" Lynne asked when Damon finished. She rolled over on her side to face him.

"I have a pretty good idea, but I need to have a few more conversations tomorrow to verify my suspicions."

"With whom?"

"If you don't mind, I'd like to prove my theory first. And get some sleep."

"You're keeping me in the dark?" Lynne asked.

Damon smiled and flipped off the lights.

Chapter 18
Saturday, January 18

Perspiration streamed in rivulets down Eric Fraser's face. Damon found the *Vitamin's* first officer pumping his limbs on a fitness center elliptical machine at eight o'clock in the morning.

Damon had tracked down Captain Harris, who clued him in on Eric's morning exercise routine. The machine next to Eric's was free.

"Can I get you a fresh towel before I get going?" Damon asked him—Eric's was soaked through with sweat.

"That would be great, thanks," the first officer replied. "You were the police inspector's witness, right?"

"I was." Damon handed Eric a dry towel, wrapped another around his neck, and climbed on the open elliptical. "It must have been pretty shocking for you and the rest of the staff."

"We see a lot of things on the ship, but that was my first suicide." Eric jabbed a finger against the console in front of him, and his machine slowed to a walking pace.

Damon glanced at the screen on Eric's machine—a five minute cool-down. He had to hurry. "Did you discuss the death with the captain and other staff?" He set his exercise machine to a slow jog.

"A bit, sure. It's only natural. Captain Harris, myself, and the second officer—Naliaka Diop—talked about it. Mainly, what we did right and how we could improve our protocols if we're ever presented with a similar situation. The captain is big on teachable moments."

"Protocols?" Damon asked.

"Working with the police, pulling up the body, coordinating with the doctor, things like that."

"Did you speak with the housekeepers about it?"

"The dead woman's stateroom attendants?" Eric looked at Damon with a combination of curiosity and annoyance. "Why would I do that?"

Damon faced straight ahead, avoiding eye contact with Eric. "I just thought you may have spoken with the women to reassure them everything was all right. Or to confirm for yourself that their room keys hadn't been taken and replaced by phonies. I'm sure you checked your own."

Fraser laughed. "You've been reading too many mystery novels. My master key has been working fine all week. And if either housekeeper had a key that wasn't opening the rooms they've been assigned, I would have heard about it by now. Besides," he said, dropping his voice, "she committed suicide."

"I know," Damon said with forced laughter. He cranked up the speed on his elliptical and broke into a run. "I just always wanted to solve a real-life mystery."

* * *

After an invigorating workout and shower, Damon made his way to the stretch of hall where Miles, Amanda, and Candice had their staterooms. He said a silent prayer that none of them would come into the corridor as he lingered, hoping to spot Eva Ricaurte or her supervisor, Daniela Montalvo. A young couple with two boys passed by. Damon pretended to admire the bland artwork hanging on the hallway wall.

Two minutes later, Daniela pushed a cleaning cart out of a nearby room. She reminded Damon of a hospital matron—thick neck muscles connected a boxy jaw to her square shoulders. The senior stateroom attendant's dark hair was streaked with gray and crimped into a bun the size of a jelly doughnut. Damon stepped in front of her cart.

"Ms. Montalvo, can I speak with you for a minute, please?"

Daniela smiled warmly. "Of course, sir. What do you need?" Her accent was heavy, but her grammar, perfect.

"I was in the captain's conference room on Sunday morning, when the police inspector asked you about your key," Damon reminded her.

A wave of recognition swept over Daniela's face. "Of course. I remember now. Poor woman."

Damon mumbled his agreement with the sentiment. "Is there someplace private we can talk?" he asked.

"Private? I don't understand."

Five doors down, a stateroom door opened, and a family of three walked in the opposite direction.

"I wanted to ask you about your key card. The one that could open Mrs. Drummiller's room."

"What would you like to know?" she asked apprehensively.

"Have you been using it all week?"

"Of course, sir," Daniela said.

"And it opens all of the proper doors?"

"The proper doors?" she repeated with confusion. Then understanding crept in. "You mean does it open all of the doors for the staterooms I clean? Yes, it has all week. No problems."

"Any problems with Eva's key?"

"Not that she's told me about," Daniela said.

"Have you tried your key on Mrs. Drummiller's door?" Damon asked.

"The *deceased* woman?" Daniela whispered.

Damon nodded.

Rather than respond verbally, Daniela removed a key card from the front apron pocket of her uniform and approached the door to Philippa's stateroom. She slipped the card into the slot and a tiny light below the handle immediately turned from red to green. Daniela pushed the door open. Before she could close it, Damon stepped inside.

"I just need to check one thing," he said.

Daniela opened her mouth to protest, but Damon quickly snapped the door shut.

Thirty seconds later, Damon was back in the hallway. Daniela shook her head at him disapprovingly but kept quiet and shoved the key card back into her apron.

"Thank you," Damon said. "You didn't let anyone into Mrs. Drummiller's room? Before she died, that is."

"No, sir." Daniela replied.

"How about any other of your rooms?"

The stateroom attendant shook her head vehemently and repeated, "No, sir."

"I'm sorry to have bothered you." Damon handed Daniela a twenty-dollar tip, and the housekeeper scooted with her cart into a nearby room.

* * *

Twenty minutes later, Damon had a nearly identical conversation with Eva Ricaurte—except she confirmed one crucial piece of information that Damon had suspected.

* * *

Damon's last visit of the morning was to the Drummiller family patriarch. After scouring the ship for an hour, he found Houston tucking into a plate of nachos at a snack bar near the ship's miniature golf course. Damon dispensed a cone of vanilla soft serve and walked directly into the big man's line of sight, feigning interest in a "closest putt" competition.

"Damon," Houston said.

Damon turned. "Hello, Houston. Fine day isn't it."

"It is." He pointed to a chair, and Damon sat on the opposite side of a red metal table.

"Makes you wish we didn't have to disembark tomorrow," Damon said casually.

Houston shoved a cheese-laden nacho chip into his mouth, chewed quickly, and swallowed. "It doesn't bother me. The whole week has been surreal with Philippa dying. In retrospect, we should've gotten off of the ship in the Bahamas and taken care of the arrangements right away."

"Why's that?"

"Not much in life scares me," Houston said and wiped a smear of cheese from the corner of his mouth with a soiled napkin. "But I find it disturbing to think about her lifeless body just a few decks below, especially when I'm up here taking in the salty ocean breeze like a man without a care in the world."

"It must be strange not seeing her with your son," Damon said and nibbled on the top rim of his cake cone, careful not to upset the balance of ice cream.

"That's for sure. It hasn't even been a week since I last saw her alive." He sighed.

"There's something I was hoping to ask you about that first day," Damon said, steadying his nerves. He looked directly at Houston. "You were in Philippa's stateroom before dinner, correct?"

* * *

Damon spent thirty minutes during the afternoon with Captain Harris. The ginger-haired captain listened patiently, made a few telephone calls, and agreed to Damon's request to post a security team in civilian clothes near Damon's table in the Pelican Room that evening.

Damon then spent the next hour in one of the *Vitamin's* computer centers. He drafted a narrative describing Philippa's death, the motives of each member of the Drummiller and Carmichael families, the details of his investigation, and finally, his conclusions. He saved the chronicle on a thumb drive he'd purchased in one of the ship's gift shops, then e-mailed the substance to his good friend Gerry Sloman. He asked Gerry—a detective with the Arlington County, Virginia, police force—to contact Miami law enforcement and request that officers meet the ship upon its return to the United States the following morning.

Chapter 19

"Have you made any progress in proving that Lucho is trying to commit insurance fraud?" Damon asked his mother.

"I did," she replied.

They were taking in the late afternoon air on their stateroom balcony. Lynne had offered to order a bottle of champagne from room service, but Damon declined, insisting he needed his wits about him for that evening's dinner—the "last supper," as they'd later refer to it.

"Lucho had no intention of cheating the insurance company," Lynne said. "To the contrary—insurance brought him down."

Damon flipped his sunglasses onto his forehead and gave his mother a sideways glance.

"Lucho was up to no good," Lynne clarified, "but the only person he was trying to con was his wife." She had an ear-to-ear grin.

"You're enjoying this, aren't you?"

Lynne nodded.

"Solving mysteries can be pretty gratifying, huh?"

"I wasn't the one who solved it," Lynne admitted. "Rudy did."

"A father protecting his daughter?"

"Something like that. I met Rudy by the pool this morning and told him the necklace Emily brought to the jewelry shop last night didn't look like Fava's. Rudy was surprised that neither of us spoke up at Hector's, but he was relieved in a sense, too. He said his gut told him all along that Jack and Fava as counterfeiters didn't seem right, and he was pleased his instincts aren't on the fritz."

"Did you tell Rudy you thought Lucho was the one who had the fake necklace made?"

"I did," Lynne said. "Much as he hated to admit that his son-in-law may have done something disreputable, that storyline made more sense to him. Then Rudy told me something interesting about Lucho. He has a bit of a gambling problem."

Damon snapped his fingers. "I knew I recognized him from somewhere. I've seen him in the casino—at the high-limit tables."

"You're not playing those are you, Damon?"

He laughed. "No way." Damon reached for a bottle of water resting on the small plastic table between them. "So Lucho has a gambling problem but wasn't after insurance money."

"That's correct. According to Rudy, Lucho and Emily are fairly well off. He's an airline pilot, and she manages an upscale restaurant."

"So what happened to Emily's necklace?" Damon asked and sipped water.

"After we spoke this morning, Rudy told me he was going to confront Lucho. He asked me to meet him in the Galleon at noon. Over lunch, Rudy told me everything."

Damon waited for Lynne to continue. She playfully plucked the water bottle from his hand and made a show of taking a drawn-out drink.

"Are you enjoying toying with me?" Damon asked in frustration.

After another minute, Lynne replied. "Just a little payback for you not telling me how you think Ernie Mencken's death relates to Philippa's."

Damon grunted. "Trust me, you'll find out soon enough."

Lynne set down the water bottle. "Rudy found Lucho having a snack in one of the cafés on the promenade and told him that Jack and Fava hadn't stolen Emily's necklace. When Lucho started to protest, Rudy explained that the pieces were different. Then he relayed the scenario we discussed: Lucho had a fake necklace made before he even boarded the ship—and speculated that Lucho made the switch to pay off a gambling debt. Rudy threatened to go to the police if Lucho didn't fess up."

"Did Lucho flip out?"

"No. According to Rudy, Lucho buried his face in his hands and had a hard time holding back tears. He admitted that his problem was more serious than anyone knew and told Rudy he'd been $15,000 in debt to a loan shark. But he swore he didn't commit insurance fraud. He couldn't have—the necklace wasn't insured."

"Why didn't he pay back the money using his salary? You said he's a pilot."

"Lucho said he couldn't—he and Emily have a joint bank account. She'd notice the missing money immediately."

"And he didn't want his wife to find out he'd lost that much."

Lynne nodded.

Damon frowned. He knew he was missing something. "So how did Lucho plan to pay off the debt if the necklace wasn't insured?"

"Rudy asked him the same question. 'I already did,' Lucho answered." Lynne laughed. "You look confused, Damon. I imagine Rudy was, too, at that point. But before Lucho told Rudy anything else, he begged him to keep it a secret from Emily. Rudy didn't agree right away. He insisted he needed to hear Lucho out before he could commit to keeping anything from his daughter."

Damon picked up the bottle of water and finished it.

"There was no counterfeit necklace," Lynne said and began to apply sunscreen to her forearms. "Actually, that's not accurate. There was no *second* necklace. The original never had a real sapphire to begin with."

Before Damon could wrap his head around the information, Lynne explained. "Lucho gave Emily a necklace for her birthday two weeks ago. It looked breathtaking, but the gemstones were fake. It cost him less than $200."

The light in Damon's head finally clicked on. "He took $15,000 from their bank account to satisfy his gambling debt."

"Exactly," Lynne said. "When Emily saw the withdrawal from their savings, she assumed the money had been spent on her necklace. Of course, that was Lucho's intent—we both heard him claim the necklace cost fifteen grand."

"So Lucho could pay off the loan shark without his wife finding out he'd blown so much money."

"You got it."

"Sneaky. So why the ruse at Shadow's Lounge?"

"Because Emily let on that she planned to get the necklace insured. A couple of days into the cruise, Emily asked Lucho if he'd gotten a formal appraisal. When he said he hadn't, she insisted on getting one as soon as they arrived back in the States to send to their insurance company. Lucho was caught off guard and knew that as soon as the necklace was appraised, he'd be caught. So he contrived the deception. He paid someone he met in the *Vitamin's* casino $500 to turn out the lights in Shadow's Lounge at a prearranged time. In the ruckus that followed, he yanked the necklace off Emily and let it drop to the floor."

Damon shook his head in disbelief. "What was his plan after that?"

"To keep quiet until Emily had the necklace appraised. She'd come home one afternoon after they'd resettled into their daily routine and tell Lucho the necklace was worthless. He'd express outrage and spin a yarn similar to the story we discussed at Braised: Someone must have photographed Emily's necklace on board the *Vitamin*, had a counterfeit made at one of the ports of call, and robbed her in Shadow's Lounge. He'd tell his wife how ingenious the thief's plan was, because once back in Massachusetts, they'd have no way to find the crook."

"But then I started talking about Fava's necklace," Damon said.

"And Lucho ran with the idea that Fava and Jack were the thieves in his storyline. He had to after you suggested we have a jeweler at Hector's look at the piece. According to Rudy, Lucho planned to speak with Jack, who would deny the accusation, then Lucho would tell Emily that he'd follow up with the police. He wouldn't of course, but he'd wait a couple of weeks and then tell Emily that the police said they didn't have enough evidence to press charges."

"Rather ingenious in a way," Damon commented. "Is Rudy going to tell his daughter?"

"He gave in and told Lucho he wouldn't as long as Lucho enrolls himself in a program to treat his gambling addiction as soon as they arrive home."

"I suppose that's the best course of action," Damon acknowledged. "Will Lucho still pretend to confront Jack tonight for show?"

"I doubt it. He may leave their table and come up to the Pelican Room for a few minutes as a pretense, but I doubt he'll even come to our table to say hello."

Damon stretched his arms above his head. "Will you see Rudy again after the cruise?"

Lynne smiled at her son. "Probably. There are airplane shuttles between D.C. and Boston several times a day. And how about you, Damon? Any plans for you and Amanda?"

"Not likely," Damon said. "Especially after we get through dinner tonight."

* * *

At 6:25 sharp, Damon and Lynne entered the Pelican Room and took their usual seats. They were the first diners at the table, and Damon used the opportunity to nod to a pair of plainclothes security guards pointed out by the headwaiter, Charles. The officers—sitting at a nearby table for two—looked like a couple on their honeymoon. They nodded back to Damon in unison.

Five minutes later, Jack and Fava approached the table. Fava was dressed to the nines—full but tasteful make-up highlighted her clear blue eyes, and a black designer dress with a plunging neckline accentuated her curves. Her dark hair was set in a French twist.

Damon looked down at his short-sleeved polo and pressed khakis. He groaned inwardly.

"You look stunning," Damon said, rising to his feet.

"Thank you," she said. "It's the last night on the ship. I might as well make the most of it."

"I'm certain it'll be a night to remember," Damon replied. As he sat back down, the Drummillers and Carmichaels filed into the Pelican Room.

"Want to have one last go-round tonight?" Amanda whispered into Damon's ear and sat to his right. She looked becoming in a form-flattering, cornflower-blue dress and knee-high leather boots.

Damon was surprised—after the previous night's conversation, he had no idea how Amanda felt about him.

"Let's see if you're still up for it after what I have to say tonight," Damon whispered back.

Amanda looked at him intensely. "What are you planning to do, Damon?" Her voice rose.

As Damon shushed her, Houston spoke to the gathering. "I'd like to thank everyone for joining us at our table this week. It certainly hasn't been easy for our family, but you all have been most pleasant company."

After a murmured round of agreement, Damon spoke up. "I'd like to order a bottle of champagne to toast our week together."

"An excellent idea," Houston said. "But it's on me." He waved Niels to the table and ordered two bottles of Veuve Clicquot.

"That's very kind of you, Houston," Damon said with a smile.

Minutes later, Kristjan poured champagne into flutes and Houston slid Niels his SeaPass card—drinks were always extra.

Champagne in hand, Houston made a toast to new friends and to mourn the loss of his daughter-in-law.

After allowing time for sips to be taken, Niels approached Houston and whispered something to him.

"Declined?" Houston said in disbelief. "There must be some sort of error. There are no limits on these cards." Shaking his head, he added, "I'll have to run down to Guest Services after dinner." He took the SeaPass card Kitty had removed from her purse and handed it to Niels.

A minute later, Kristjan brought appetizers to the table, and Kitty signed for the champagne—her card didn't have any trouble.

Damon allowed another fifteen minutes to pass. After Niels and Kristjan served entrées, he tapped a butter knife against his water glass. Conversation stopped and everyone at the table looked at him. Damon cleared his throat, then said, "I'd appreciate if everyone could indulge me with a bit of your time. I have a confession to make."

Chapter 20

"A confession?" Houston parroted. "Let's hear it."

Damon cleared his throat. "I've been investigating every one of you."

"Whatever for?" Kitty asked cautiously.

Damon delivered the news plainly. "Philippa didn't commit suicide. She was murdered."

Houston and Miles both jumped to their feet. "What the hell are you talking about?" Houston shouted. Kitty shushed her husband. He sat and waved Miles down to his seat. "Why on earth would you say such a vile thing, Mr. Lassard?" Houston said through gritted teeth.

"Because it's true."

Houston opened his mouth to protest, then shut it. Damon looked around the table. Kitty's eyes were cast down toward her plate, as were Miles's. Raymond turned up his nose, smiling with smug satisfaction; his wife appeared perplexed. Lines of anger crossed Candice's brow. Amanda looked more curious than anything else.

Jack broke the silence. "A real-life murder mystery? Now I've seen it all." He looked at Damon. "Don't keep us in suspense, young man. Let's hear it."

Fava turned to Jack. "This sounds personal. Perhaps we should leave," she said unconvincingly.

Jack shook his head furiously. "No way I'm missing this."

All eyes turned toward Damon.

"I've believed since day one that Philippa had been murdered," Damon started. "That's why I've been so interested in the Drummiller and Carmichael family histories. I wasn't just being nosy, I was looking for information that would explain not only who killed Philippa but why."

"This is ridiculous," Miles objected. "Philippa committed suicide. The inspector found a note—you of all people should remember. You were in my wife's room when he found it."

"I remember all right," Damon replied. "But the note itself suggests that Philippa was murdered."

"How?" Candice asked. Her anger had turned to fascination. "Her room was locked. And none of us have balconies."

"I still can't believe the ship screwed that up," Houston grumbled. "It makes me feel like I'm trapped in a—"

"First," Damon interrupted, "the note was typed. That in and of itself doesn't point to murder, though a note handwritten by Philippa would have been more definitive of suicide. Second, and what seemed particularly interesting to me, is where Inspector Albury found the note."

"The inspector said it was in her nightstand," Amanda said. "That seems like a pretty normal place to leave a suicide note."

"Perhaps," Damon conceded, "though lying on the top of the nightstand or bed would seem more likely than in the drawer. But what I found remarkable is that Inspector Albury found the letter tucked underneath the Bible, not on top of it. So even if Philippa had opened the drawer, she wouldn't have seen the note."

"He didn't tell us that," Amanda said.

"I noticed," Damon replied. "So the question becomes, 'Why would Philippa hide a suicide note?' The answer? She didn't. The murderer knew the police would thoroughly inspect Philippa's room and find the note, but he—or she—needed to make sure Philippa didn't come across it before she met her demise. Philippa wasn't a religious woman, was she Miles?"

"No," he said flatly.

"So as long as the killer knew she wasn't likely to pick up the Bible, the note was nestled in a safe spot."

"Hold your horses," Houston said. His face had turned scarlet. "As long as the killer knew she wasn't religious? It sounds to me that you're suggesting one of us here at the table killed Philippa!"

"Shush," Kitty whispered to her husband. "Don't make a scene."

"Don't make a scene? Lassard here is accusing a Drummiller of murder!"

"A Drummiller or a Carmichael," Candice corrected.

Vicky whipped her head toward Candice, bearing her teeth.

"One of you at the table did murder Philippa," Damon said quietly. "And I know who."

"I've had enough of this," Houston growled. "I'm going to get security."

"They're right behind you, Mr. Drummiller." Damon pointed to the nearby officers who appeared to be listening intently. "I suggest you calm down."

Jack spoke as Houston clenched his teeth. "You're suggesting the murderer was in Philippa's room before she was killed, right? Because if he went in after the fact, he wouldn't have to hide the note. He could have, as you said, left it on top of the nightstand or the bed."

"That's correct," Damon said. "The killer was in Philippa's room prior to meeting her behind the aquatics theater in the early-morning hours on the first night of the cruise. In fact, the killer was in her room twice. But I'll get to that a bit later."

"Why would someone *murder* her?" Fava asked. Damon could see by the gleam in her eyes that she was keenly interested. *She craved excitement*, he thought.

"Every single member of the Drummiller and Carmichael families had a reason to kill her," Damon said. "First, there's Miles."

Damon preemptively held up his hand, and Miles pursed his lips.

"One can always find a reason for a husband to kill his wife," Damon continued. "Not only did Philippa emasculate Miles, but he also found a woman he may have preferred to her."

Damon turned to face Vicky. "That's you, of course."

She turned crimson, and twisted away from Raymond.

"The morning I witnessed the search of Philippa's stateroom, Inspector Albury first knocked on Miles's door to notify him of her death. Miles wouldn't let us inside, and I suspected he had someone in there with him." Damon looked from Vicky to Miles and back again to Vicky. "I take it by your silence that I am, indeed, correct. It's no secret. I believe everyone in the family knows."

Miles stared at his plate of halibut.

"So Vicky had ample motive to do away with Philippa, too," Damon said. "To marry Miles, assuming she could rid herself of Raymond first."

Damon picked up his champagne flute, looked Fava squarely in the eye, then set it down again. Instead, he sipped from his water glass. "As for Raymond, I was curious why he would agree to come on this cruise. He was Houston's and Kitty's godson, and they paid for the trip, but why spend a week with your wife and her paramour? Raymond answered that question when he tried to smuggle a pickle jar full of redback spiders onto the *Vitamin* in Saint Thomas."

"That's poppycock," Houston said. "Raymond missed the boat."

"Fibbing won't you get you anywhere, Mr. Drummiller," Damon said. "I spoke with one of the security guards who detained Raymond. I suppose you didn't want the family name besmirched by any sort of scandal. Well, after tonight, you can forget about that."

"Is that a threat, Mr. Lassard?" Houston barked.

"No." Damon steadied cold eyes onto Houston. "Just a fact."

To his left, Damon heard Fava purr with excitement.

"I couldn't prove in a court of law why Raymond brought those redbacks onto the ship," Damon continued. "But I'm fairly certain it was to poison his adversary, Miles."

Raymond winced under Miles's daunting glare.

"Whether Raymond thought the spider bites would kill Miles or just paralyze him, I don't know. But I believe he's harboring a potent mix of animosity and jealousy. Miles's dalliance with Vicky was only one fork leading to Raymond's hatred. The other was more deep-seated—Miles snatched the large grocery-chain client Raymond was pursuing while he was still working for Drummiller Box and Board. Along with the client, Raymond lost a stake in the company and the respect of his godfather. Powerful stuff."

Raymond picked up his butter knife, then laid it back down on the table. "However I feel about Miles, or Houston for that matter," Raymond said quietly, "has nothing to do with Philippa."

"I agree," Damon said. "If Miles and Philippa had been in love, I could see someone exacting vengeance on him by killing her. But I don't think Miles is losing too much sleep over Philippa's death."

"You seem to have dirt on everyone," Candice said with a devilish smile. "How about me, Damon? Do you know my dirty little secret, too?"

"Yes," Damon replied with sympathy. "I know your mother forced you to terminate your pregnancy against your wishes."

Fava gasped.

"Well done," Candice said. "Are you a detective back in the real world?"

"Not yet, but I'm working on it," Damon replied. He turned toward Amanda. "You had the most to lose financially. Philippa was making a play for her and Miles to appropriate your share of the family trust."

"Daddy never would have done that to me," she protested.

Houston nodded genially at his daughter. "That's right," he said.

"That's easy for you to say now that Philippa's not in your ear," Damon said.

Houston made a guttural sound.

"It sounds like you have the goods on everyone but Houston and Kitty here," Jack said.

"No, I have information on them, too," Damon replied. "I know Kitty thought Philippa was beneath the Drummillers in terms of social status. And Houston has more than one secret."

The security guards at the next table leaned in close.

"What, pray tell, are these secrets?" Houston demanded.

"There are two. One pertains to you and Philippa, but I'll leave it—that doesn't bear on her death. The other secret, however, provided the impetus for her murder. Or to be more accurate, disclosure of the other secret."

"You're talking gibberish," Miles groused.

"I'm happy to explain," Damon said. "When Houston started his box-making business, he had two partners: Zach Bristol and Ernie Mencken. He bought Zach out of the business fifteen years ago, but poor Ernie met a harsher fate."

"We all know about that," Miles said. "Ernie died in a fire,"

"Zach and I were lucky to survive," Houston said gruffly.

Damon ignored Miles and Houston, and recounted the story Amanda had relayed to him, including Houston's role in setting a fire to torch the evidence of Ernie's white-collar thievery. He noted that the partners had turned off the sprinkler system—it hadn't malfunctioned. Then he walked step by step through the events that Houston witnessed before the fatal match was struck: Zach Bristol knocking out Ernie and locking him in a supply room, sealing his fate.

Houston glared at Amanda, then Miles, then Kitty. He knew one of them had betrayed his confidence. Candice's mouth hung open. Raymond's smile stretched from ear to ear—he was relishing the death spiral of the Drummiller dynasty.

"Whether this story is the entire truth, or Houston played a larger role in Ernie's death and its cover up, I don't know," Damon said. "But that's the account Houston gave to several of his family members, including Philippa, when he thought he was dying of colon cancer. I suspect that after Houston recovered, he realized he'd made a serious mistake. Philippa tried to blackmail you, Houston, didn't she?"

"I don't know what you're talking about you little SOB," Houston countered. "I suggest you watch your mouth before I have my lawyer slap you with a suit for slander."

Damon pressed on. "That's why you started leaning toward moving Amanda's share of the trust to Miles, and in essence, to Philippa. To keep her quiet. I wouldn't be surprised if she was pushing for a lump sum immediately, too. But even if you paid her off, you couldn't be sure Philippa wouldn't still notify the police. You may not have locked Ernie in the supply room, but knowing he was in there when you and Zach set the fire would be more than enough to bring permanent shame on the Drummiller family."

"Regardless of what you say, Mr. Lassard," Houston snarled, "I didn't murder Philippa."

"I know," Damon replied. "Your wife did."

Chapter 21

Kitty's head was bowed, her fingers interlaced in front of her face. Fleshy thumbs pushed against the bridge of her nose.

Damon shot a quick glance at Houston. The elder man's eyes were glazed, like a boxer who'd just taken a right cross. "Even if Philippa was paid and elected not to tell the police," Damon said, "she could always come back demanding more assets. Or splash the story all over the front pages of the newspapers. But Kitty wouldn't let that happen. She'd do anything to protect the Drummiller family name. And she did."

"Ridiculous," Miles said. "My mother wouldn't hurt a fly and all you have, it seems, is a whole lot of conjecture."

"Perhaps as to the precise motive, but what isn't supposition is how Kitty carried out her plan."

"This ought to be good," Jack said with spirit.

Raymond sniffled. *Kitty was probably the only person at the table*, Damon thought, *he cared for more than superficially.*

"The murder was premeditated," Damon said. "Kitty took at least one, and probably two, steps before she boarded the *Vitamin*. First, contrary to popular belief among everyone here, the ship's booking agent did not make a mistake by assigning Philippa a room without a balcony. I asked Captain Harris to make some calls. Kitty booked the trip for the entire family. Records in the cruise line's reservations department show Kitty specifically requested that none of the rooms she booked have a balcony. She wanted the police to be sure no one could have entered Philippa's room without her permission if the doors were locked. The reservations department also had a record of Kitty's request that Philippa's room connect with Amanda and Candice's room rather than Miles's. She had a good reason for that, which I'll get to in a moment."

Damon took a breath. "The other thing I suspect Kitty did before boarding is type up and print out the suicide note. Theoretically, she could have drafted and printed it in one of the ship's computer centers, but that would have been risky. So armed with a note and Philippa's stateroom set up to her specifications, Kitty was prepared to carry out her daughter-in-law's death sentence."

Kitty rubbed her eyes. They looked raw. Houston laid a hand on her back.

Damon sipped water, leaving his champagne untouched. "On Sunday afternoon, shortly after boarding the *Vitamin*, Kitty and Houston went to Philippa's stateroom. Kitty contrived a reason, something about a magazine she loaned Philippa on the plane and wanted to retrieve to read poolside."

Kitty glanced at her husband. He caught her eye and mouthed, "Was that a secret?" Over his plate of nachos earlier in the day, at Damon's prompting, Houston had described the quick stop he and Kitty had made to Philippa's room on the first afternoon of the trip.

"While she was inside," Damon said, "Kitty managed to unlock the interior door that joined Philippa's stateroom to Amanda and Candice's and tape back the bolt. That way, if Kitty was able to access Amanda and Candice's room later, she could pass into Philippa's room unimpeded."

Houston shot his wife a look that Damon couldn't interpret.

Damon imagined the scene: Kitty making a pretense of examining the interior door and applying the tape, using her girth to prevent Houston and Philippa from witnessing the maneuver.

"You can't prove any of this." Miles declared.

"This morning," Damon said, "one of the stateroom attendants let me into Philippa's cabin. I found and photographed small remnants of a piece of masking tape near the bolt of Philippa's interior door. Inspector Albury only checked the handle; he never looked at the bolt."

Damon looked around the table. Every diner was focused on him, seemingly spellbound. "On Sunday evening, while dinner was wrapping up after Jack bit into the shard of glass"—Damon paused and allowed a grimace to creep onto his lips—"Kitty asked everyone at the table what their plans were for the evening. The question seemed innocuous, but she was intent on knowing when Philippa, Amanda, and Candice would be out of their rooms."

Niels and Kristjan came to the table to clear plates but drew back, undoubtedly sensing tension in the air. Damon waved them closer. As the waiters bused the table in silence, Damon watched Kitty closely. Mascara smeared the wrinkles under her eyelids, and her jaw began to spasm.

After the waiters departed, Damon said, "A stateroom attendant let Kitty into Amanda and Candice's room at ten thirty on Sunday night. Kitty used the pretext of delivering a bouquet of flowers to Candice for her birthday."

"You used me?" Candice said quietly to Kitty. "I thought the florist delivered those."

"Shut up, Candice," Houston said.

Eva Ricaurte had confirmed Damon's suspicions. On the first night of the cruise, while the rest of the

Drummiller family was enjoying the *Vitamin's* entertainment offerings, Kitty had positioned herself in the hall in front of Amanda and Candice's room, bouquet in hand. She waited for a housekeeper and when she spotted Eva, Kitty asked to be let in. She explained that it was her granddaughter's birthday and she wanted to surprise her with flowers. Eva was hesitant—housekeepers aren't supposed to allow guests into any other passenger's room. But Kitty showed Eva her SeaPass card. Her last name matched Candice's, so Eva opened the door for her.

"Once inside the room," Damon said, "I believe the following sequence of events took place. Kitty dropped the flowers on the dresser, along with a 'Happy Birthday' note to Candice. Then she unlocked the interior door on Amanda and Candice's side, wedged it open, and pushed through the door on Philippa's side. The masking tape did its job. She planted the suicide note under the Bible in Philippa's drawer, and left a second note—addressed to Philippa—inside the room as well. It asked Philippa to meet her, presumably behind the aquatics theater at a designated time during the overnight hours. I found remnants of that note in Philippa's clothing in the ship's medical center. I suppose Kitty could have slipped the 'meet me' note under Philippa's door at another time, but as long as she was inside, she probably left it then—most likely on the floor near the front door. Had she left it anywhere else, Philippa would have known someone had been in her room."

Damon politely waved away Kristjan, who had approached the table with dessert menus, then continued. "After Kitty left the suicide note and the 'meet me' note, all she had to do was unpeel the tape from the bolt on Philippa's interior door and step back into the adjoining room, pulling Philippa's door closed behind her, which snapped the bolt shut. That's why, when Inspector Albury checked the handle of Philippa's interior door the following morning, it was locked. Kitty then shut the interior door of Amanda and Candice's room and walked out their front door. That way, if Eva was still in the hall, she would have seen Kitty exit Amanda and Candice's room, not Philippa's."

Damon paused for breath, then added, "The 'meet me' note I found was waterlogged and largely unreadable. I suspect it suggested that Kitty wanted to discuss a payoff in exchange for Philippa's silence about Houston's involvement in Ernie Mencken's death. When Philippa arrived at Kitty's chosen location near a secluded guardrail, it would have been a simple matter for Kitty to surprise her with physical force and cast her overboard."

Damon had played out the scene in his head, filling in language from the 'meet me' note with his imagination:

Philippa and Miles enter their separate staterooms at twelve fifteen, after parting ways with Damon and Lynne at the Crooner on the first night of the cruise. Philippa notices a slip of paper just inside her door as she flips on the overhead light. She picks it up. A woman's script. She reads: "Zach Bristol killed Ernie, no one else. Your repeated threats of going to the police and the press are wearing thin. Let's agree on a fair sum that will shut you up. Meet me on the shuffleboard court behind the aquatics theater. Two a.m. tonight. After that, I never want to hear a word about this again."

Philippa smiles to herself. Finally, she'll have a real payday.

She changes into a blouse, cardigan, and jeans, then waits patiently, the television on mute. At one o'clock, she can hear muffled voices next door in Miles's room. Vicky coming to make love to her husband. Homely old Vicky. Gross. If Miles wanted a lover, couldn't he find someone more attractive? He had enough money—why not pull in a looker like the woman Jack Jackman brought on the cruise? She shuddered at the thought of Vicky and Miles embracing on the other side of her stateroom wall. Not because she cared—she'd never been physically attracted to Miles and hadn't allowed him to touch her body in years—but the thought of Vicky being intimate with any man disgusted her.

At 1:50, Philippa slipped out of her stateroom. She crumpled up the note and shoved it into the front pocket of her jeans. Kitty was already at the shuffleboard court when she arrived, leaning against the railing at the back of the ship under a solitary light.

Kitty pushed herself away from the rail as Philippa approached and turned to one side in a gesture of disrespect. Philippa stepped around her, placed one hand on the guardrail and slowly twisted her body until the women stood face-to-face, less than twelve inches apart.

"How can you live with yourself?" Kitty hissed. "Blackmailing your own in-laws?"

Philippa's nostrils flared. "It's not hard."

"Everything you've ever had is thanks to the determination and good graces of my husband and son."

"That may be, but I've had to live with that windbag for over twenty years. Now, are you ready to talk turkey?" Philippa's eyes glistened with greed.

"I don't think so, my dear." Kitty shifted the weight of her body into Philippa, pushing her up against the railing. Philippa opened her mouth to shout, but Kitty clamped a hand over it. With the other, Kitty pried Philippa's hand from the rail.

"Too bad you never learned to swim, Philippa dear," Kitty said with a fiendish grin. Then, with all of the strength she could muster, Kitty pushed hard against Philippa mouth and used her opposite forearm to scoop Philippa under her rear and tip her overboard.

Philippa screamed as she fell, but her voice was subsumed by the sound of waves crashing against the hull of the Vitamin. In the moonlight, Kitty watched her struggle, Philippa's arms flapping like a baby bird's wings. As she gulped down mouthfuls of water, she began to sink, then minutes later, her body resurfaced as a floating corpse.

Damon looked up at Kitty. She was sitting as still as a scarecrow, expressionless.

"Your story is outlandish," Houston said, "and any evidence you have is circumstantial, Mr. Lassard."

"But it all points in one direction," Damon replied. "To Kitty. There's one last bit of evidence I'd like to review." Damon crooked a finger in the direction of Niels, who was waiting nearby.

"Niels, may I see the receipt for the champagne that Mrs. Drummiller signed at the beginning of dinner?" he asked as the waiter stepped toward him.

Niels quickly retrieved it. Damon inspected Kitty's signature on the receipt as well as the numerals she inserted for a tip and final cost. Then he pulled a sheet of white paper from his pocket and unfolded it on the table next to the receipt. "A photocopy of the 'meet me' note," he explained. Captain Harris had allowed Damon to retrieve the note from Philippa's clothing and make a copy of it. The original was being stored in the captain's personal safe. Kitty had made a mistake writing the note by hand.

"Is that why my SeaPass card didn't work?" Houston grunted. "You offered to buy champagne but knew I'd insist on paying. Then you had my card disabled so Kitty would have to sign for it."

Damon nodded. "The authorities will want a formal handwriting analysis conducted, of course," Damon said, "but the penmanship on the receipt looks similar to the writing on the note, even with the smeared ink."

Lynne and Amanda leaned in close on either side of Damon to look. Fava craned her neck to do the same. All three looked up at Kitty simultaneously.

"Grandmother, how could you?" Candice roared.

"Now, now," Miles said. "Candice, calm down. The company has a team of attorneys. We'll get the best criminal-defense lawyer possible."

"You're defending her?" Candice shrieked at her father. "She killed your wife! My mother!"

Kitty buried her face in her hands and started crying. "All I've ever wanted to do is to protect my husband. My family."

Houston patted Kitty's shoulder. "Don't say another word, dear."

The *Vitamin's* two security officers rose from their nearby table. They led Kitty out of the Pelican Room with Houston and Miles in tow.

Damon explained to those who remained that he'd provided a chronicle to a police detective in Arlington, Virginia. Gerry Sloman had replied by e-mail to Damon shortly before dinner—he'd passed Damon's information to his counterparts in Miami. A team of police officers would meet the ship when it docked in the morning and arrest Kitty on charges of murder before extraditing her to the Bahamas.

After dessert, Damon and Lynne said their good-byes. Jack, who either didn't realize that Damon and Lynne had been the ones to put the kibosh on his ploy or didn't let his animosity show, shook their hands vigorously.

Fava looked at Damon with admiration, then moved her mouth close to his ear. "My real name is Aubree Graham. Look me up if you ever come to Dallas." She briefly touched her wet lips to his earlobe. Damon shivered with a mixture of excitement and repulsion.

Vicky bid them farewell cordially. Raymond's focus was elsewhere as he shook Damon's hand, muttering, "I can't believe it was Kitty."

Candice smiled at Damon. "Thank you," she said with sincerity. "I didn't get along well with my mother, but she was my mother. At least I know she didn't commit suicide, so I won't have to wonder why for the rest of my life." She exhaled. "I'm glad it's over."

But it was far from over, Damon knew. There would be lawyers and newspaper reporters to face as well as testimony and a trial in Candice's future. He didn't envy her.

Amanda shook Damon's hand stiffly. "Good-bye, Damon," she said with a formal tone. He gave her an apologetic smile, and said, "sorry," knowing there would be no final rendezvous with her.

"I suppose you did what you felt needed to be done," Amanda replied. "But now my sweet mother will spend the rest of her life in prison, and our family will be outcasts in Raleigh-Durham. And for what? No one liked Philippa." She bit her lower lip. "It wouldn't have hurt anyone to just let sleeping dogs lie." She turned and walked away.

Damon felt a pang of guilt dart through his chest. Did solving Philippa's murder help anything other than his own sense of pride? He shook his head and pushed any self-reproach to the recesses of his mind. Candice was better off knowing how her mother died. And surely Philippa had other relations and friends who had the right to know the truth.

* * *

"Do you think she'll be convicted?" Lynne asked Damon once they were safely back in their stateroom for the night.

"Gerry thinks the likelihood of putting her away is high. He told me in his e-mail that I'll have to testify at the trial."

"That should be exciting."

"Good training, too."

"And what about Houston—will he be in any trouble with the police?"

"Gerry wasn't sure, but he passed along the information I gleaned from Amanda about the insurance fraud and Ernie's death to the police in North Carolina."

Chapter 22
Sunday, January 19

The *Vitamin of the Seas* arrived in the Port of Miami at six o'clock in the morning. Damon stood alone on his stateroom balcony. Lynne was still sleeping. Nine decks below, three Miami police department squad cars sat at the front of the parking lot. Damon watched four uniformed officers board the *Vitamin*. Two others leaned against one of the cruisers, drinking coffee. Ten minutes later, Kitty Drummiller emerged at the top of the gangway in handcuffs, escorted by the Miami police officers. Houston and Miles trailed the cluster marching off of the ship.

Once they reached the pavement, a balding man in a dark suit emerged from a black sedan. He shook hands with Houston and Miles, then spoke briefly to Kitty and the officers. *A defense lawyer,* Damon thought. Houston had probably called ship-to-shore after dinner the previous night.

Kitty was guided into the back seat of a police cruiser while her husband and son joined the suit in his sedan. The cars crawled in a funeral-style procession out of Damon's line of vision.

* * *

"So what did you think of your first cruise?" Lynne asked Damon as their airplane's wheels lifted off of the ground.

"Not quite as relaxing as I'd imagined," Damon said.

Lynne patted his arm. "You were very clever. You're going to make a fine police officer. And I have no doubt, you'll be a detective before you know it."

Damon smiled and closed his eyes. Three weeks until training began. After the week he'd been through, Damon felt sure he could handle anything.

THE END

ABOUT THE AUTHOR

 STEPHEN KAMINSKI is the award-winning author of the Damon Lassard Dabbling Detective Mystery series published by Cozy Cat Press. The first two cozy mysteries in the series are "It Takes Two to Strangle" (2012) and "Don't Cry Over Killed Milk" (2013). Stephen is a graduate of Johns Hopkins University and Harvard Law School. He currently serves as an executive with a national non-profit organization.

www.ingramcontent.com/pod-product-compliance
Lightning Source LLC
Chambersburg PA
CBHW020322260626
47156CB00004B/1337